I0835735

ROLL AGAINST
Betrayal

ALLYSON LINDT

ACELETTE PRESS

This book is a work of fiction.

While reference might be made to actual historical events or existing locations, the names, characters, places and incidents are either the product of the author's imagination or are used fictitiously, and any resemblance to actual persons, living or dead, business establishments, events, or locales is entirely coincidental.

Manufactured in the United States of America

For my eternal dragon…
and every reader who's been with me since my first
3d20 book

Sydney fumbled with a wire shelf for her booth display. This was normally a two-person job, but if she could just twist her arm in one direction and snap the securing clip in by reaching around and under…

Her phone chimed with a new text, startling her, and her grip slipped. She maneuvered herself into the right position again and let out a pleased yelp when the fixture snapped into place.

She grabbed her phone. The message was from Kim.

I can't make it this weekend. Family stuff. Super sorry.

Sydney snarled at the text. Because of course, when she hired Kim to help her at the convention and asked, *Are you sure you don't have any issues with this being over the Labor Day weekend,* she'd taken Kim's *I'll be fine* at face value.

All wasn't lost yet. Unlike the last several cons

Sydney exhibited at, this one was in her hometown. She had to have at least one friend who could hop in to help her out.

She sent out a series of texts and emails, and returned to setting up the framework for her booth while she waited. As one reply after another rolled in, her frustration grew. Everyone was either working tomorrow or already out of town. One person said they might be able to pop in for a few hours on Sunday, but they weren't sure.

Sydney had the rest of today to get the booth set up, and she could do that on her own. It would take more than twice as long, but she'd manage. Surviving a three-day con without help, though? That was going to suck.

Just thinking about it made her want to double up on the coffee. Which was a good idea. She needed a break anyway.

She padded through the brightly-lit convention center, her sneakers scuffing softly on the concrete floor. Most of the concessions weren't open yet, since the event hadn't started. The one coffee shop that was had a line that grew out the door and wrapped around a couple of pillars.

It was a good excuse for her to take a longer break.

Most of the people in line were on their phones, but she was caught up on her email for now, and wound too tightly to scroll through social media.

A squeal echoed through the halls, and a couple of cosplayers in their mid-twenties ran past. One wielded an ax as big as she was, while she chased her friend.

The people around Sydney were dressed more like she was—jeans, T-shirts, and sneakers. The *I expect to get dirty* uniform of the veteran vendor. Snippets of conversation drifted toward her: speculation about whether the show would clear one-hundred-thousand attendees, people wondering if they'd brought enough figurines, and exclamations of disgust and awe about how much celebrity autographs were going for this year.

Sydney loved the energy that hummed through the room. Her game, *Changelings and Caverns,* started as a way for her and her friends to spend weekends being geeky but in a new way. Like any of their favorites, the setup involved figurines, a board game, and a lot of roleplaying.

Sydney tweaked and modified the rules until it morphed from a knock-off to its own unique experience. Then she'd gone out on a limb and had a few hundred copies of the game manufactured.

What started as a labor of love had turned into a revenue stream for her. She was still thrilled every time someone bought a copy of C&C. Attending fantasy cons and comic cons all over the country, to get the word out, was an added bonus.

She also liked seeing new places and people. For instance, the sexy guy who just moved into view a few people back in line. His dark hair was trimmed short, and the faint scruff of beard was kind of sexy. Like really sexy.

As in, she should probably stop staring. Or take one of those sneaky pictures. She could send it to Kathryn and share the love. Remind her best friend how much she was missing out on, despite being at the lake with her two boyfriends.

Yup. Two. And Sydney had a hard time keeping one. Go figure.

She tried to be subtle about angling her phone up, making it look like she was just checking something at a really high angle. She clicked the button to take the pic, and the flash went off.

Fuck. He looked up and met her gaze for a blink, before she ducked her head and dropped her phone into her purse.

Fortunately, the line chose that moment to inch forward, taking him out of her line of sight.

Despite almost getting caught, she was tempted to glance over her shoulder for another look. Instead, she ordered her iced coffee—extra espresso and sugar—and moved to the other side of the counter, to wait.

The staff was working quickly, and drinks came up for the people ahead of her in rapid succession.

"Excuse me," a sexy voice said. "May I borrow your phone?"

Was he talking to her? She looked up, and her pulse kicked up at the sight of Sexy Guy, who was apparently the owner of Sexy Voice. He watched her, the corners of his dark brown eyes crinkled in amusement.

"Is yours broken?" She mentally facepalmed. *Real smooth, Syd.*

"Nah." It came out like *naw,* with just a hint of a drawl. "But I don't need pictures of myself. Seems like you do."

She was glad she wasn't a blusher, because with the heat racing under her skin, she'd be bright red. "I wasn't..." She couldn't force the denial out.

"My mistake. I'm Dylan, by the way."

"Sydney."

"Pleasure to meet you." He shook her hand. His grip was warm and firm and sent delicious images dancing through her head. Fantasies of what else he could do with those hands.

"Same." She forced herself to speak. No other words came, though. She wasn't so great at small talk with strangers. He was going to think she was a dolt.

"What are you selling?" he asked.

The question didn't attach to a point of reference, and she stared back blankly. "Excuse me?"

"Your booth." He nodded at her badge. "What are you selling?"

"Oh. Board games. You?" Crap. That was her opening to give him the snappy elevator pitch about her game and impress him when she said she was the creator.

He thumbed his lanyard to spin his badge around.

It had the huge *Volunteer* stripe down the side. "Myself, I suppose." Was he flirting?

"Right. Of course." Why couldn't she carry on her half of this conversation? "What are you volunteering, besides time? I mean... I promise I usually make more sense. Do you get to meet anyone famous?"

Every time he smiled or laughed, the corners of his eyes crinkled. It was cute plus sexy, and that was a lethal combination. "That remains to be seen. Are you famous?"

I'm hoping to be. The words stuck in her throat.

"Iced coffee. Extra sugar and shot. For Cindy." The barista called.

Sydney gave Dylan a regretful smile. "That's me. It was great meeting you. Enjoy the con."

She grabbed her drink, and as she strolled away, her mind treated her to an instant replay of every moment in the conversation when she could have been wittier. Handing over her phone to a stranger seemed like a dumb move, but if he'd taken a picture, she could have asked him to include his number along with it. Or asked how much he charged, if he was the product. Or anything more interesting than, *Do you get to meet anyone famous?*

Fantasizing about Dylan would keep her company tonight, but for now, she needed to finish setting up her booth.

DYLAN WAS INTRIGUED BY THE WOMAN WITH THE RED and blue Harley Quinn pigtails and the shirt that said GEE*K IS S*EXY. The way her hips filled out her jeans and her breasts stretched the letters on her Tee was sexy. If he could get her over the nervousness, the conversation might be even better.

It might not be, but the only way to find out was to keep her talking.

Too bad she was gone.

He snagged his iced tea when it was ready. As long as he was here, he should roam the vendor hall floor. He'd scored the volunteer badge by writing up the legalese for the convention—policies on harassment, cosplay, weapons and the like—and it gave him permission to wander anywhere not marked *Private*.

An unforeseen and fantastic side-effect of passing the bar a few weeks ago.

He'd wanted to be a lawyer since he was a kid. His friends played fireman and astronaut, and he acted as an arbitrator when they fought. Kind of boring-sounding when he looked back on it, but he enjoyed it. When his grandmother died, several years back, she'd left most of her savings to him. It wasn't enough to make him wealthy, but she'd asked he use it to pursue his dream, and he had.

Her money took him through pre-grad. Working for the biggest corporate-contracts law firm in the city had covered the rest.

Dylan headed into the main convention hall. He'd never seen it this way before. This wasn't his first convention, but he'd only been an attendee in the past.

The various booths sat in different stages of completion, and it was neat to see. Some spots, the vendors had finished assembling and setting up already. Others, people scurried around with boxes and dollies, setting up. Most of the booths were still curtains and cards with company names that would be occupied by later today.

He turned down another aisle and approached a larger booth, filled out with wire displays, similar to what many vendor tables would look like in twenty-four hours.

And there was Sydney. The view was just as fantastic from behind, and he trailed his gaze along her curves as she reached up to place an uncooperative box on a higher shelf.

He hurried to her side and grabbed the lagging end. "Let me help."

Working together, it was a simple task to secure the limited edition Sephiroth motorcycle.

"Thanks." Her shy smile returned when she looked at him.

He tried to help with the awkwardness by glancing around the booth. "Are you here alone?"

"I don't have a boyfriend." She covered her face. "Oh God." Her hands muffled her voice. "I'm such an idiot."

He tugged her wrist, so he could see her again. When he was younger, he got in trouble for not thinking before he spoke. Since then, he'd learned to make it work for him. For the most part, what came out of his mouth was best left unfiltered. "Nah. You saved me a question. Let's get this out of the way up front, and maybe it will help. Yes, I'm flirting."

Shock spread across her face. That meant she wasn't hiding anymore. She glanced over her shoulder, then back at him. "Me?"

"Yes. Now that we've covered that, are you working the booth alone? Do you need more help?"

"With my flirting, apparently." Her laugh was hesitant but melodic. "And help would be wonderful. My assistant bailed for the weekend, and I thought I could handle things, but if you're offering, I'm accepting."

"Point me in a direction, boss."

She gestured to a middle section. "Boxes are stacked by order they go up. Make things look nice and neat on the shelves."

Simple enough.

He went to work. After a couple of minutes, he glanced over his shoulder, to find Sydney watching him.

"Enjoying the show?" he teased.

"Yes, but no. But yes. I… You didn't ask any questions."

"About the work? Seems pretty straightforward."

She smiled and turned to her own section.

He tried to start a conversation a few times, but

the tearing of tape and boxes and the clatter of shelves kept cutting him off. That was a shame.

He finished his tasks and found her arranging the front table with several boxes of *Changelings and Caverns*. "Is the game that good?" he asked. "I mean, good enough that it dominates your display."

"It's a fantastic game. And I'm not just saying that because my company makes it."

He was glad to hear it. She probably didn't care what her boss did with the intellectual property, but Monday morning, Dylan was meeting the guy to negotiate a more robust publishing and distribution deal with one of his clients. This would be a good chance to get to know the product better.

A short while later, they wrapped up. She stepped into the aisle and surveyed the entire booth. "It looks fantastic. Thank you. I would have been here all day if you hadn't come along."

"Glad I could help."

She wiped her sleeve across her forehead and grimaced. "I'm all gross. I need a shower. You could help with that, too." Her scowl deepened. "That was over the top, wasn't it? I was joking."

"You're putting too much thought into it." He was glad to see her more comfortable around him. He was enjoying her company, despite not having exchanged many words with her.

"Is that a tip from a professional flirter?" she asked.

He grinned. "First lesson is free, and after that… Yeah, never mind. I have no idea where that's going."

Her laugh came more easily this time. "So even the smooth and suave Dylan fumbles sometimes."

"All the time." He didn't have an issue admitting that. "You said your assistant bailed for the entire weekend?"

"Yes."

"Do you want me to stop by for a couple of hours tomorrow and help you out?" He was here to enjoy the con, and if things went well with Sydney, he could add hot, naked, orgasmy enjoyment to the list. Or at the very least, a geek-reference-filled afternoon of fun.

"I can't ask you—"

"Let me stop you there." He held up his hand. "You didn't ask, I offered." He thumbed his badge out. "Volunteer, remember? Would you like my help? *Yes* or *no*."

Her smile was back. "That would be fantastic."

"Great. I'll see you tomorrow." He leaned close. "Enjoy the shower."

She shook her head and stepped away. "Nope. That's definitely too much. It says *needy*, and that's not how you strike me."

"Touché." He gave her an exaggerated bow. "Until then."

Dylan was grinning as he strolled out to the underground parking lot.

His phone rang. It was his roommate, Josh.

"Hallo," Dylan answered.

"How quickly can you get online? We had a senior partner fuck up a contract, and I need to know what you remember."

Dylan groaned. He didn't need to ask which partner. "I'll be home in half an hour."

If Josh ever found a magic lamp, he was pretty sure he'd wish for an always-full mug of coffee.

On mornings like this, he'd make copious use of it.

He stifled a yawn and inched forward with the rest of the line in the espresso bar. After staying up until nearly three with Dylan, ensuring the corrupted contract literally had every *i* dotted and every *T* crossed, Josh needed something stronger than what the pot at home offered.

Dylan—lucky bastard—had the week off. So he was in the hotel room he'd reserved for the con, and was probably sleeping his day away. He and Josh had been roommates the beginning of law school. They'd both graduated since, but paying student loans on a junior lawyer salary meant splitting the rent still made sense.

As the queue crawled forward another person,

Josh checked the time on his phone. The law firm where he and Dylan worked was a few floors up in this building, and Josh had plenty of time before he had to be up there, but he wanted to get to his desk before anyone else came in. He had research to do.

It didn't matter that Josh's last name was on the firm marquee—his grandfather founded the group, and his mother was one of the current senior partners—he wasn't afforded any leeway.

Unlike the asshole partner who caused so much work for them last night, and would slide under the radar because he was fucking Josh's mother.

"Next," the girl at the register called.

He stepped forward with a smile. "Hey, Luci. Mocha Red Eye. As big as it gets."

"TGIF?" She marked his drink order on a cup, then handed it to the barista.

"So very much. But Comic Con this weekend."

She laughed. "Do you do the whole dress-up thing?"

"No. I like to let the world revel in my natural awesomeness."

"That's very noble of you. Catch you Monday?"

"Of course." He stepped aside, so the next person could order.

He'd miss the rituals here. The people. The coffee. But he couldn't wait to get out of this place. Law might be the family tradition, and he liked practicing, but this firm wasn't for him. He did his job because it was his job. His other plans were why he'd gotten to the office early, though.

"Extra-large Mocha Red Eye," the barista called. He was a new guy Josh hadn't met yet.

Josh would know his name in a week or so. He grabbed his drink and headed for the elevator. A few minutes later, he settled in at his desk. Half the lights in the place were out, and no one else had arrived yet.

It was time for research. The firm represented a large game distributor, who specialized in tabletop and roleplaying games. The distributor wanted to acquire rights from the local company that had created *Changelings and Caverns*. Josh had maneuvered his way into working with the client. His goal was to meet some people, make some connections, and move into a new role, in a very different industry.

Part of that good impression would be learning everything he could about them, in order to represent them properly.

He used to make up games like C&C with his ex-girlfriend, and he'd loved it. She was the creative one; he was more about helping her grow her ideas. He wanted to do more of that. Help someone with a talent like hers expand their products and reach more customers.

He tumbled down the research rabbit hole, not emerging until the chatter grew around him. The office was bright now. Most desks occupied. Phones ringing. People shouting information at each other.

The rest of his reading would wait until later. He

dove into work, pulling files, doing legal research, typing up documents to file with the courts—whatever anyone needed.

His phone rang, and *Laurie Hunter* flashed on the display. His mother. "Hello, Ms. Hunter," he answered. He never called her *Mother* at the office. It was almost TV-show cliché.

"I need to shift your priorities, Josh." Her tone was cool and professional. "We're working on new boilerplate language for Automan Life, and I want you to shadow the lead attorney. To learn, and also to double-check their work."

"What am I handing off in return?" The moment he asked, he knew the answer.

"The Polar Bear negotiation. Dylan will step into that spot instead. You can fill him in, but I need you on Automan. I trust you to do this."

Josh liked her confidence in him but didn't care for the news. "I can do both."

"No. I'm sorry. I need you focused on Automan. I know you were looking forward to working on the other, but you're going to be stretched thin as it is. In fact, I need you to take Saturday to come up to speed. Your meeting with them is Monday."

Well, fuck.

"But I was going into Tosche Station, to pick up some power converters!"

"You can waste time with your friends when your chores are done."

The lines from Star Wars echoed in his head, but

he resisted the urge to launch into them to make a point. So much for catching Comic Con with Dylan.

He sent his roommate a text. *Working this weekend. If you hook up, don't be stingy with the details.*

The new contract information was already waiting for Josh in his email. He clicked into it and dove in.

SYDNEY WAS BRACED FOR A LONG DAY OF SOLO-PLAY. Hanging with Dylan yesterday was fun, but she didn't expect him to be back.

That was all right. His flirting was enough for her to feed her fantasies last night and expand it into a vivid scene. One where they did end up in the shower, slipping and sliding against each other, water cascading around them as he knelt at her feet and licked her to orgasm, then bent her over—

A throb pulsed between her legs, and she squeezed her thighs together. Thoughts like that needed to wait until she wasn't about to be set upon by crowds of people.

"Where do you want me boss?" Dylan asked.

She started when she realized he was behind her, and not in her head still. "Hey." Great. Now she'd forgotten how to speak again.

"You look surprised to see me."

Sydney shrugged. "It's nothing personal. Most people wouldn't come back, and I don't know you well enough to bank on anything else."

"Let's change that." He stepped into her booth. "First, tell me what I need to do."

She could do that. She gave him a rundown of pricing. She'd handle the money. "No offense," she said.

"None taken. I understand earning trust, and this is someone's livelihood."

People were starting to wander the aisles. Not a lot—the doors opened an hour early for gold-pass members—but enough that Sydney felt like she should focus on them instead of the hottie standing next to her, arm brushing hers every couple of minutes.

A group of three walked by, their gaze drifting to the table.

"Do you like games?" Sydney called.

They broke eye contact and hurried away quickly.

There would be a bit of that this weekend, but it was disheartening to start Day One off that way.

A pack of five girls in their late teens wandered past. "You ladies like to have fun?" Dylan called.

They exchanged looks and giggles. "Yes," one said.

"We've got an assortment." He nodded to the shelves behind him.

"No thanks," another replied. They walked away, glancing back until they rounded the corner.

And then someone said *yes*. Before they finished their transaction, another person was waiting to buy a game.

It didn't take long before Sydney and Dylan had their hands full, bagging purchases, making change, and answering questions.

When there was a lull in the crowds, as new panels started, Sydney sank into her seat. She was grinning, despite her aching feet.

"This is insane." Dylan shifted his weight. "Do you do this a lot?"

"Every weekend there's a big enough convention."

He shook his head. "I don't know if I'd love that or hate it, but I wouldn't mind giving it a try."

"What's your favorite flavor? Fandom, I mean?"

He furrowed his brow. "I have to pick? All of the above." He gestured to the room.

That was so vague. Sydney wanted to keep chatting, but someone else was looking at her C&C. "Do you like games?" she asked.

The woman, who was dressed in an intricate Poison Ivy costume that left little to the imagination, skipped forward. "Love them. You?" Her voice was low and sultry, as she spoke in-character.

"Yeah. Absolutely." Sydney grinned. "What's your favorite kind?"

Ivy licked her lips. "Anything with vines or tentacles." Wow. She did the whole roleplaying thing beautifully.

"Sounds kinky." Dylan chimed in.

"It is, handsome. The kinkier the better. You two like to party?"

Not really. The answer died on Sydney's lips when Dylan said, "Depends on the party."

Ivy handed him a flier. "Upstairs, after everything shuts down tonight. They'll ID you, and there's a cover charge."

"We'll see if we can make it." Dylan took the leaflet.

Ivy strolled away, hips swaying.

Sydney glanced over Dylan's shoulder. The invitation was photocopied black text on green paper. It looked like a generic invitation, covered with cosplay clip art, including a maid costume, handcuffs, and a whip.

Dylan glanced at her. "Could be fun. Want to be my date?"

There was no way she was turning that down. "Sure."

Something brushed her leg, and she swatted at it without thinking. A second brush, this one harder, pressed in on her leg, and she looked down to see her cashbox gone.

A short, thin guy crawled out from the other side of the table and ran into the crowds.

"Fuck," she shouted. "That kid just stole my cash box."

"I'll be back," Dylan yelled over his shoulder. He was already chasing the cash box thief.

The aisles were crowded, making it difficult to move. The kid was at least a foot shorter than Dylan and wove through people's legs, knocking several off balance.

The thief was pulling ahead, and frustration spilled through Dylan, mingling with adrenaline. He shouted "*Move*," and earned a couple of dirty looks and several laughs for the command.

And then he spotted an opening between booths, thanks to a group of people in costumes, getting their pictures taken. He darted between tables, behind the curtains that divided one aisle from the next.

Debris spilled into his path, but he hopped over it and emerged on the other side, ahead of the kid.

He grabbed the thief by the arm. "Give back the box.'

"Get your hands off me, you freaking pedo-bear," the kid screamed.

Sure. *Now* people turned to look.

Dylan wasn't taking this bullshit. "Give me back the cash, you little thief."

"Is there something wrong?" A volunteer approached.

Dylan recognized one of the security guys, not only from the shirt that said *Security* on the back, but they met during orientation yesterday.

"Jesse, hey." Dylan tightened his grip when the thief struggled and tried to jerk away. "He stole the cash box from one of the vendor booths."

"I found it on the floor." The kid hugged his prize tighter. He couldn't be more than twelve or thirteen.

Jesse extracted the box from him and handed it to Dylan. "You'll make sure it gets back safe?" Jesse asked.

Dylan nodded.

Jesse escorted the kid toward the exit.

With the show over, everyone turned back to what they'd been doing. Dylan's pulse still raced through his veins, and in a few minutes, the adrenaline would start to sit heavy in his gut.

He made his way back to Sydney's booth. He would have chased the thief anyway, but her smile when she saw him was the perfect reward.

Dylan handed her the retrieved box. "I'm pretty sure he didn't have time to open it."

"Thank you, thank you." She turned it over in her

hands. "Nope. Lock is still intact. Did I say *thank you*? I can't believe you did this for me."

He gave a deep bow and tipped an invisible hat. "'Twas my pleasure, m'lady."

"Hey, man. That was awesome, what you just did," said a male voice.

Dylan turned to see a couple of guys waiting to shake his hand. He obliged. "Thanks. I hate it when anyone thinks they can get away with that shit."

"Totally." The second guy picked up one of the C&C boxes. "I've heard about this. Is it any good?"

"It's the best." Dylan had spent a little time last night researching, and it looked like a lot of fun.

"I'll take it." The guy handed over money.

For the next bit, people who heard what Dylan had done trickled in. The constant traffic drew additional attention, and they sold several copies of the game.

As the crowds thinned again, Dylan finally had a chance to breathe. He looked at Sydney, who was flushed but smiling. "I don't know how you do this all the time," he said.

"I love it. But it's also not usually this busy. You're my lucky charm. Either that, or I've used up all my good karma for the next year by meeting you."

"Something tells me you have more in reserve." He had a hard time imagining there were many red marks in her ledger.

"You shameless flatterer." Her shyness looked exaggerated.

He liked seeing her relaxed—the way she moved, her smiles, those gorgeous, full curves. "I'm being sincere."

"Excuse me. When you two are done hanging off each other?" an irritated woman interrupted.

Sydney clenched her jaw.

"I've got this," Dylan said softly enough only she would hear. He faced the woman. "May I help you?"

"Are you the asshole who tackled and assaulted my boy earlier?"

Great. He was dealing with the brat's mother, apparently. His defensiveness cranked several notches. "Since I didn't tackle or assault anyone, no. Was it your kid who stole my boss's cash box?" He wanted to toss back the insults, but if he was being approached this way, he wasn't giving her any legal footing.

"He found a box on the floor and picked it up. He didn't know what was in it. Next thing he knew, some maniac was chasing him and threatening him."

"Witnesses say differently." Irritation flipped a *play it cool* switch in Dylan's head. He would freeze this woman out one way or another.

"Are you calling me a liar?"

Dylan shook his head. "No. I'm calling your son a liar."

"Absolutely ridiculous. Slanderous, in fact. I'm going to sue you until you can't spin without running into a wage garnishment."

She'd gone there. Dylan hid his smugness. "That

doesn't even make sense. But you do that." He pulled his wallet from his pocket and plucked a business card out. "You can reach out to my employer directly. They'll represent me."

She paled when she looked at the card. "You don't work there."

"Then you humiliate me by sending any legal papers there. Give it a try and see. I'll be waiting to be served at that address."

"Fine." She jammed the card in her purse and stalked away.

Who needed coffee, when there was this much excitement in the day? Dylan's heart hammered against his ribs at the confrontation. Or rather, the lack of a resolution.

He wanted to demand she come back so he could finish the conversation. Logic her into a corner she couldn't outrage herself out of.

She'd been bluffing with the lawsuit comment, so he'd never see her again. That was the most disappointing thing of all. That kid would keep pulling the same bullshit until his mother wised up or someone else stepped in.

Sydney was grateful Dylan dealt with the irate woman. Confrontation wasn't her forte.

When Dylan handed over a business card, Sydney's gut twisted in on itself a second time. The

Hunter & Associates logo was one she'd never forget. Her ex's mother had drilled that family legacy into Sydney's head repeatedly.

"You work for Hunter & Associates?" She made sure to keep her voice steady. This wasn't worth overreacting to.

He nodded. "Just moved from paralegal to attorney."

"Congratulations. Do you like your job?"

He shrugged. "It's pretty decent. They gave me the weekend off, to hang out here, and I can't complain about that."

"I guess not." She smiled. Sydney wouldn't say anything negative about the firm. She had her issues with *Ms. Hunter,* but if Dylan was happy there, she wouldn't drag him down with her bias.

She needed to shake off some of this excess energy. "I'm going to take a break. Are you okay to watch the booth for a few minutes?"

"You trust me here with all of this?" He gestured. "Alone?"

Maybe that was naive of her, but she did. "You had a chance to rip me off and didn't. Plus, I know where you work," she teased.

"Take a break. I'll hold down the fort, boss."

Walking away was its own kind of stress. She left assistants with the booth at every show, but she didn't know this guy, and it was too easy to like him.

As she wove through con-goers, her thoughts cleared and calm returned. She didn't want to leave

Dylan alone for long, but she paused at a few booths, to appreciate the unique art and designs.

The brief stroll was enough to refresh her. She paused at a food stall on her way back. When the woman asked her what she wanted to drink, she stalled on an answer. What did Dylan like, besides coffee? She got two Mt. Dews and hoped for the best.

As Sydney approached her booth, her footsteps slowed. Dylan was talking to a woman in yellow vinyl hot pants and a matching sleeveless top with a red shirt thrown over it. The character was Faye from Cowboy Bebop, and the woman made the outfit look better than Poison Ivy had earlier.

Faye laughed at something and rested a hand on Dylan's arm. He was grinning, eyes bright and posture casual. They stood close, and whatever they were talking about, the conversation flowed easily.

Sydney swallowed the rush of jealousy. What did she expect from the bold, flirty, gorgeous guy who was too good to be true?

She pasted on a smile, hoped it didn't look too fake, and joined them.

Dylan's smile when he saw Sydney warmed her.

It's not the same smile he's giving Ms. Gorgeous.

Right.

"I promise I wasn't slacking." Teasing lined Dylan's voice when she drew within earshot.

Sydney made her mask-smile even wider. Was she overcorrecting? She probably looked like she was grimacing. "No worries. I'm not a total slave-driver." She forced a chuckle.

"No? Shame, he might like that." Ms. Gorgeous nodded at Dylan.

He rolled his eyes but looked amused. "Tori, this is my temporary boss, Sydney. Syd, this is my cousin. She's heading up the cosplay parts of the con. Got me the volunteer gig."

Cousin. Of course. *Could I be anymore cliché?* But Sydney couldn't ignore the relief that flowed through her. "Nice to meet you."

"Same." Tori trailed her gaze over Sydney. "He's right. You're cute, in that sexy-vixen kind of way. Do you cosplay?"

He told someone that about her? "Not really." She didn't care if other people ignored body-type for a costume, but she'd never been comfortable squeezing into spandex bodysuits or short skirts.

"You should. I'll hook you up sometime. And I'm sorry to meet and run, but I'm supposed to be in a panel soon. Nice meeting you," she said to Sydney. "I'll call you later," she called over her shoulder to Dylan as she walked away.

Less than a day into the actual con, and this was already one of the more random shows Sydney'd ever been to. She was good with that, as long as more of the random leaned toward *complimentary friends and family* and farther from *cash box thieves and their over-protective mothers*.

The rest of the day was uneventful, beyond the fact that Dylan was an incredible salesman. Sydney didn't know the last time she'd had such a good first day. She was looking forward to heading up to her hotel room—she always got a room, even for local shows, because it was less stressful than commuting—and curling up with a book, and maybe some fantasies about Dylan.

He held up the flier Poison Ivy gave them earlier. "You up for a party?"

She'd forgotten about that. Her instinct was to say *no*. She definitely wasn't a party person. That it was him asking made her hesitate. "Sure. I could do that for a little while." Except not like this. She was dusty and sweaty. "If there's time for me to clean up first."

Maybe she shouldn't have said that. He had to be local if he worked for Hunter & Associates. Would he get bored, waiting for her? Decide it was easier to go home?

Why couldn't she shut her brain up?

"I doubt anyone is going to care if we're not there right when things start." Dylan's reply saved her from her thoughts. "Meet me back in the lobby in an hour? Is that enough time?"

It was probably too much. Her head would think her into a million different scenarios between now and then. "Thirty minutes?"

"Even better. Until then." He grasped her fingertips and kissed the back of her knuckles.

Heat flooded under her skin until she thought she might combust. "Until then." Her reply came out as a squeak.

The next half hour crawled at a snail's pace and moved at lightning speed simultaneously. Sydney took the quickest deep-scrub shower in history. *Everything* had to be scrubbed and pristine and flowery-smelling.

Her hair would have to stay pulled up, though. Washing and drying it took eons.

She stood in front of her luggage, shaking her head at every piece of clothing she'd brought. Why did she have to be such a practical packer? It was all jeans and T-shirts. Not even notable ones. All of it meant to be comfortable for a day of standing around and working.

At least she'd brought cute panties. Not that it would matter, but her imagination had already jumped ahead several hours. On the teensy, tiny chance he wanted to stick around for the night, she'd be happy she had the cotton bikini briefs with the subtle Wonder Woman logo on the left hip.

Or was that stupid? Did she wish she'd brought lace?

"Shut up, brain," she said aloud, to kick herself out of her head.

When she was finally ready, there were eight minutes left of her thirty. She sat on the edge of the bed. How long did the elevator ride down take? If she left now, would she be too early? She didn't want to keep him waiting, but she didn't want to appear over-anxious.

Why not?

Good question. Was it such a big deal if he thought she was eager?

She was looking for reasons to procrastinate. She grabbed her wristlet and headed downstairs.

Dylan was already in the lobby, and he flashed her

a drop-dead sexy smile when she caught his eye. "You ready to see what all the excitement is about?" he asked.

"Now's as good a time as any."

He produced the flier from Poison Ivy, noted the room number, and a moment later, they were knocking on the door to the second-floor suite.

"Hey. You made it." Ivy opened the door enough to see them. The room behind her was dark. "Before I let you in, you have to promise you're both over the age of eighteen and that you're not easily offended."

Odd disclaimer.

Dylan glanced at Sydney, and she shrugged. "I promise," she said.

"Me too. Adult. Not easily offended."

Ivy's smile grew, and she let them in. The suite connected to another, and the entry between was open. Faint flickers came from the other rooms. "Contemporary and school girls behind me, occult and fantasy in the other living room, and tentacles in the second bedroom. Take your pick. It's like Las Vegas—what happens here, stays here. Enjoy." She winked.

Tentacles?

"What's your poison?" Dylan whispered, his breath hot against Sydney's cheek.

"Occult and fantasy?"

He rested a hand at the small of her back and steered her toward the adjoining room.

The TV on the far wall was playing anime. A flush

covered the priestess' cheeks, and a pixelated penis was thrust into her mouth.

Correction, they were playing hentai—anime porn.

In the room, a couple sat on the couch, and another in the chair next to them. A girl was reclined in the corner on a beanbag. They were all in various states of undress, groping themselves and each other while the video played.

Heat spilled through Sydney's veins.

"Pick a room or leave." An irritated woman's voice came from behind.

Dylan pressed his frame into Sydney's back, nudging her out of the doorway. His hard length pressed into her ass.

He was turned on by this? Then again, the throb and growing dampness between her thighs confirmed she was too. Not because of the cartoon. Rather, the people in the room, exploring each other, not caring who watched, had her pulse hammering in her ears and her nipples straining against her bra.

Dylan brushed the edge of her ear with his lips. "Do you want to stay?" His question was so soft, she barely heard it.

Yes. *Fuck* yes. Arousal and curiosity kept her feet to the floor. Propriety and everything else she'd ever experienced told her this wasn't where she wanted to be. Would he stay without her if she said *no*? Make himself comfortable with the solo girl with the blue hair, whose gaze kept flicking to them as she pushed her shirt up to tease her breasts through her bra?

"Do you?" Sydney asked.

He slid his hands to her hips, then forward along her pelvis. "I'm thinking about it. But not alone."

"Maybe for a little while."

"Is that a *yes*?"

She nodded.

He leaned against the wall, tugging her with him, her back pressed to his chest, and he wrapped his arms around her waist.

"Kind of hot, isn't it?" His voice was still low, not meant to reach beyond her.

Cartoons fucking? Not her thing. Though she was a teensy bit captivated by the priestess, who seemed to be enjoying sucking on one pixelated man while another penetrated her from behind.

"The potential audience, that is." Did his voice just drop an octave?

She didn't have an extensive sex life of experience to draw on, but she had her fantasies. One she'd only ever told Josh about, and loved to fall into alone, was being on display—knowing someone was getting off watching her do the same.

"Yes." Her reply came out a dry squeak, and she licked her lips.

Blue was watching them rather than the TV, her eyes wide and her bottom lip caught between her teeth. She worked one breast free from her bra and teased a thumb along her nipple.

Sydney's imagination was running rampant with fantasies of Dylan, stripping her down in front of the private group. Teasing her until she begged to come. Of him, freeing the erection that teased her back and letting her wrap her lips around it.

There was no way she could do any of that. It was called *fantasy* for a reason.

The need thrumming under her skin and the subtle sway of his hips nudging her insisted she take the opportunity if she had it

Dylan traced his mouth up the side of her neck, not making contact but leaving a trail of temptation in his wake. He nipped her ear with his teeth, and her desire spiked. "*God,* I want to find out how wet you are," he murmured.

Fear stole her voice, and need hammered at her skull. The atmosphere in the room erased a layer of her inhibition. If she said *no* and walked away, how badly would she regret it?

Maybe she wouldn't. She could always play out the *what if* in her head, on her own time.

But she wanted to find out for real. She undid the button on her jeans and pulled down the zipper, intently aware of Blue's eyes on their every move.

Sydney covered Dylan's hand, eliciting a groan, and guided it under her panties.

"*Fuck,* Syd." He pressed his lips into her shoulder and moved his hand lower.

Blue watched them, lips slightly parted, and

mimicked Dylan's motions, dropping her own hand into her pants.

Sydney gasped when Dylan dipped between her legs. The couple in the chair turned in their direction, and her heart leaped into her throat.

They wore soft smiles.

Holy fuck, she was really doing this. Not that anything was visible, but—

Dylan brushed her clit. "You're soaked. You like being a show?"

"Yes." So much better than in her head.

He teased her swollen button, caressing it until she thrust against his hand, then easing off. The heat of their audience's stares burned through her.

A new wave of boldness surged inside. She hooked her thumbs on the waistband of her clothes, and pushed her jeans and panties down, just enough to put her pussy on display.

"Fucking hell." Dylan bit her shoulder. He stroked her clit faster, and she closed her eyes, falling into the sensation.

He hit the right angle, and climax sparked inside. She bit the inside of her cheek, to keep quiet, but a moan slipped out anyway.

Dylan pushed her past orgasm, rubbing as she pushed into his touch. He eased off as the thrust of her hips slowed.

Her eyes fluttered open.

They still had a captive audience.

"I want to feel your lips around my cock," Dylan said.

The heady buzz of coming lingered in her head. She'd let him strip her naked and fuck her bent over the back of the couch right now, if he asked. She spun to face him, showing her bare ass to the room.

A loud hammering on the outside door screamed through the room, and her hammering heart threatened to burst through her ribs.

"This is the hotel manager," a man called. "Can you open up, please?"

Dylan had never seen a group of people yank their clothes on so fast. Not that he spent much time around large groups of naked people.

"We've had some complaints about activities in these rooms." The hotel manager's voice drifted in.

"I… We're not doing anything wrong." Ivy's earlier confidence was gone.

Dylan felt bad for her. Being sexy and flirting with other con-goers was one thing. Facing down an authority figure was an entirely different beast.

It was going to be tough for Dylan to think through his hard-on, but it was going limp anyway. Talk about a mood-killer. He needed to step in.

"You can't be doing… certain activities… in here," the manager said.

Dylan looked at Sydney. Her bottom lip was

caught between her teeth. "Should we go?" she mouthed.

"Soon." He couldn't listen to this. He joined Ivy. "Is there an issue?" Dylan asked.

The hotel manager paled and took a step back. "We've had complaints."

"Plural? That sounds serious." Dylan kept his tone even and cool. "What kind of complaints?"

"Well… that is, someone said there were… things going on. Look at the way she's dressed." The manager nodded at Ivy.

She wrapped her arms around herself and ducked her head.

Dylan hated that someone had tattled. "Her clothing isn't in question. This is a private room. The young lady is current on her account, isn't she?"

"I…"

"Yes or no?"

"Yes." Some of the confidence returned to Ivy's voice.

"And there's no damage being done to the room. We're not making excessive noise," Dylan said.

The manager worked his jaw up and down. "But there are things happening."

"Things." Dylan let disdain leak into the word. "Consenting adults, watching movies and enjoying each other's company? Those types of things? Tell you what. How about you give the police a call? Ask them to remove us from the premises. Make sure to tell them to bring multiple cars, so they can transport

everyone. I'm sure no one will wonder about the paying guests, being escorted from the grounds because you don't like the same kind of movies we do. And I'm certain Corporate won't mind the multiple phone calls tomorrow, from our attorneys, as we seek damages for mental pain and anguish."

The manager clenched his jaw. His face matched his red vest. "If I get so much as a hint of a complaint about noise or damages, I'm coming down hard on you."

Dylan swallowed a response to the innuendo.

"I understand," Ivy said. "Is there anything else?"

"No."

Ivy gave the manager a sweet smile and closed the door on him. She whirled to face Dylan and threw her arms around him. "Thank you." She pressed her lips against his neck.

He politely but quickly extracted himself from the embrace. "I'm here with someone."

"Oh." Ivy's face fell.

Dylan turned to Sydney, who watched with an unreadable expression. He wrapped an arm around her waist. "Thanks for the evening," he said to Ivy. "It was… exhilarating. But we're going to go finish someplace more quiet."

Sydney leaned into him as they walked from the room. They passed an empty alcove in the hallway, where the ice machine was tucked away, and he pulled her in. Pressing her to the wall, he trailed his lips along the edge of her ear. "That was wicked fun."

She sighed. Her curves molded to his body, teasing and tantalizing. "Turns out I don't mind sharing my knight in shining armor, under the right circumstances."

"I don't have anyone extra in my hotel room, but if you want to pick up where we left off…" He let the implied offer hang between them. *Fuck,* he hoped for a *yes.* Even this basic contact had him hard again. Images of her full lips wrapped around his cock danced in his thoughts. Fantasy mingled with the reality of what she'd let him do—literally gotten off on—in front of the small audience.

"The gold-pass people are allowed on the vendor floor at eight. I have to be up early."

That sounded like a *no.* "Should I walk you back to your room and leave you for the night?"

"*No.*" She winced as the sharp word slipped out. "I'd love to join you. I'm just letting you know I have to be up early."

"That's fine." He grabbed her earlobe between his teeth and tugged. "I wasn't going to let you sleep, anyway." He tilted her chin up with his finger and crushed his mouth to hers. He glided his tongue along the seam of her lips, until she parted them and let him in. Heat roared through him, pulsing under his skin and wanting to be closer.

It took immense effort to break away. "We should go," Dylan said. "I don't think Mr. Hotel Manager will be so willing to walk away if he finds us out here."

"Probably not."

He slipped a hand in her back pocket on the walk to the elevator. When a car stopped, there were three people inside. He led Sydney to the back corner and slid a hand under her shirt, to rest on her stomach. She leaned more of her weight against him.

The group wasn't paying attention to them, but if anyone turned around, they'd get a hint of a show. Dylan slid his hand higher, to tease Sydney's nipple through her bra.

She ground her ass against him, and his dick whimpered for release.

The lift stopped, and the other people got out. As the doors slid shut again, Dylan tugged down Sydney's bra, to cup her bare breast.

"Aren't there cameras in these things?" Despite her question, she leaned into his touch.

"Probably. Do you want me to stop?"

Her, "*No,*" was breathless.

When they reached his floor, he helped her straighten her clothes and led her to his room. He didn't know what it was about her that made the reckless behavior so tempting.

It was probably because *she* was so tempting. Fun. Desirable…

The instant the door closed behind them, he cupped her face and kissed her hard. They should move further into the room. He was enjoying her soft gasps and the way her hip ground against his erection too much to break away. Even for a heartbeat.

"You said something about picking up where we left off?" Sydney's tone was soft, but desire lit up her eyes.

Did he? All the blood had rushed from his head. "That sounds familiar."

She watched him through her eyelashes, holding his gaze as she knelt in front of him. Her wide-eyed, eager innocence pulsed through his veins and hammered in his ears. She dragged down his zipper and licked her lips.

Fuck. Was that a conscious reaction? Her fingers were hot against his cock when she worked him free, and he groaned.

Dylan couldn't take his eyes off her. She flicked out her tongue—a light, playful lick—and he jerked. When she took him in her mouth, he almost came.

She continued to watch him as she swallowed his length. A lock of hair fell over her eyes, and he brushed it aside. He wanted to see those captivating eyes.

He rocked his hips against her face, moaning louder as she sucked and licked along his shaft. She stroked his balls, and they tightened at her touch. He was so close to climax, but he wanted more. It was a good thing he'd stopped at the hotel drugstore for condoms before she came downstairs.

Dylan pulled away from her with immense reluctance and was greeted with a pout.

"Is something wrong?" Teasing lined her question.

He grasped her hand and tugged her to her feet.

"Everything—this entire night—is incredible. But I need to fuck you." He led her to the bed.

The instant he let go of her arm, she wrapped it across her chest, half covering herself, and ducked her head. He reached for the light switch, and she stopped him.

"You don't need to turn that on." Shyness replaced her playfulness.

"I don't have to, but I'd like to." He gently pulled her arm down. "I want to see you. *All* of you. Reality tends to be much better than fantasy."

She caught her bottom lip between her teeth. "You've been fantasizing about me?"

"Since I saw you in the coffee shop." He hovered his mouth millimeters from hers.

Her gasp was more of a suggestion than a sound. She closed the distance between them, giving him the softest kiss. "Me too." Her breath was hot against his mouth.

"Lights on?"

She hesitated, then nodded.

Dylan flipped the switch. He laid a series of light kisses along her mouth, and down to her jaw and her neck, while he glided his hands under her shirt and up her side. He yanked her top off, and she hugged herself.

He lowered her hands and dragged his gaze over her body. "I like what I see. So fucking gorgeous." He kissed along the top of her breasts, teasing her nipples through her bra. "Everything else off, too," he said.

Sensuality laced her movements, as she stripped down to nothing. "I can't be the only one who's naked."

"That sounds fair." Dylan made quick work of discarding his clothes. "Lie on the bed."

He rolled on a condom, nudged her legs apart, and knelt between her thighs. "Fucking stunning." He lowered his head and drew one nipple into his mouth. When he wrapped his tongue around the swollen bud, she squirmed. When he scraped his teeth over the sensitive skin, she pressed into his mouth and his leg.

He wanted to spend all night exploring her, but he was ready to burst. Drawn-out play could happen next. He fisted his shaft and hovered at her opening before thrusting inside.

Sydney's sigh and the arch of her back added another layer to his need. Her pussy was tight and slick, gripping him and drawing him in. Her face was screwed up with pleasure.

He'd missed seeing that in the hentai room, and was glad to get a glimpse now. "Finger yourself." He wanted to watch her get off, and it was already taking more focus than he had, to keep from coming.

She slipped her hands between her legs. When her inhibitions faded, it was clear she liked putting on a show.

Dylan was good with watching or participating.

With each stroke, she dipped low enough to brush

his shaft, until her motions grew shorter. Her gasps mingled with his grunts.

The flutter of her eyelids was enthralling, but the way she clenched his cock when she came was better.

Her hand fell away to grip the sheets. Her screams said she was still lost in climax.

Pressure built inside, narrowing his focus until he and she were the only things that existed.

Orgasm tore through him. Stars sparked behind his eyelids, as he slammed against her. He pounded until he was spent, and even then, was reluctant to slow.

He finally stopped and pressed his forehead to her chest.

The sounds of heavy breathing mingled with the whirring of the air conditioner.

Dylan kissed up her breastbone, to her mouth. "Incredible," he murmured against her lips.

Her giggle was soft. "You really are."

He stripped off and disposed of the condom, then fell into bed and pulled her back into him. His mind skipped along the next couple of hours. Maybe a shower to clean up, and using that time to explore her curves and find out what other buttons she had.

Dylan didn't know why she had this impact on him. He wasn't a stranger to a random hookup, and he didn't have the kind of skeletons in his closet that made him cringe away from a longer relationship.

But he barely knew Sydney.

She was fun. Sexy. Witty. Different.

Maybe he did know why he was drawn to her.

"When do you have to be up?" he asked.

"Seven-ish? I need an hour to get ready, get downstairs, and make sure the booth is set up."

"Stay here tonight."

She snuggled back into him and pulled his arm more tightly around her. "You got it, boss."

He liked that. They chatted, but the drowsiness in her voice was obvious.

Dylan wasn't aware he'd fallen asleep, until the jarring of the mattress dragged him back to consciousness.

"Fuck, shit, God damn it." Sydney's muttered curses pulled him further awake. She was yanking on her clothes, like she couldn't wait to get out of here.

"Syd? What's wrong?"

She didn't look at him as she slipped on her shoes. "I need to go. I can't believe— *Fuck.* I have to go."

When Josh finished law school, he'd hoped to serious cut back on weekend research.

Some things would never change, though. He'd spent his Saturday morning balancing the contract he'd been pulled from and learning about the one he was assigned to instead.

As he headed out for a late lunch, he was satisfied with the progress he'd made on both.

He was caught up enough to take Sunday off, and there was a spare key for the hotel room he and Dylan got for the con, waiting for him.

Josh had the windows rolled down on his Honda, as he followed traffic out of downtown. The sun was shining, the weather was mild, and he was going to enjoy the fuck out of the next thirty-six or so hours of his life.

He'd sent Dylan a couple of texts, to let him know

he was on his way. There was no answer, but that wasn't a big deal. Dylan would get to them when he had time.

They'd take in the con, and at the same time, they could brainstorm how to get Josh in front of the game publisher.

Josh hit an open stretch of road and smiled at the breeze floating through the car. He turned up the radio.

In law school, he and Dylan had played a couple sometimes. Sometimes for the shock value or to prove a point. Other times because a couple made a better impression at a social event. Both of them were bi, and comfortable with the masquerade of being together, so it wasn't a big deal.

JOSH WAS TEMPTED TO DO THE SAME THING NOW. IF HE were Dylan's boyfriend, it would be an excuse for them to both be at dinners with the client.

There was a huge issue there. Everyone at work knew better, and that complicated things.

The screech of tires drowned out the music. Metal and glass shattered.

Josh's skull slammed into the headrest, and his airbag pressed him tighter into his seat.

His ear were ringing. What happened?

The way his car had spun, and the shape of the passenger side—curved around a pickup truck—said he'd been broadsided. They were in the middle of an intersection.

He gingerly rolled his neck as the airbag deflated. Was he supposed to stay seated if he had a concussion? What about for whiplash?

Not really something they taught in law school.

He stretched his limbs as he climbed from the car. *Phone.* He needed that. It was still in its cradle, attached to the dashboard.

Good fixture.

He dialed 911 and stumbled toward the truck.

The other driver wore a scowl as he stepped onto the pavement. The instant he saw Josh, he started shouting. "You asshole fucking prick. Where the fuck were you going? You shouldn't have been in that intersection, you cunt."

Great. This was what Josh wanted to deal with. It added to the throbbing pain in his skull. He spared the man a glance. "Just a moment, please. I'm on the phone."

"Emergency services. What's your emergency?" a woman asked over the line.

"I'd like to report an accident at the intersection of 3900 South and Main Street. Two cars. At least two adults—"

"I'm talking to you, you pussy twat." The guy slapped Josh's hand aside, knocking the phone away.

"And I'll talk to you once I know someone has been dispatched to deal with this." Josh was so tempted to deck this asshole. He didn't want to bruise his knuckles, though. His skull screamed with every new sound, and his ears chimed like an elementary school bell at recess.

"Why the fuck weren't you watching where you were going?" At least the guy had a limited cursing vocabulary. When he stepped closer to Josh, alcohol rolled off his breath and clothes.

Awesome. Not.

Josh was going to ignore him. He crouched to pick up his phone, and the guy kicked it away.

Josh rolled his eyes. He breathed deep and pushed calm through his veins, then stood. "You ran a red light. You struck the side of my car."

"F'ckin asshole."

"Yeah. That's me." Josh kept his posture loose and his voice calm. Inside, every inch of him was prepared for the inevitable escalation of this conflict.

"Smartass." The guy swung.

Josh stepped out of arm's reach. It was a sloppy punch, and the guy's momentum propelled him a few steps past Josh.

Josh didn't want to do this. It wouldn't diffuse anything. But calm resolution didn't seem like an option anyway.

The guy let loose a rambling string of gibberish scattered with foul language, and charged Josh.

Josh sidestepped again, grabbed the guy's arm, and twisted it behind his back. Apparently he did have an everyday use for that black belt in Aikido.

The guy jerked against Josh's grip, and Josh let go.

He didn't want to break his arm or make him even madder by pinning him down. Someone might actually get hurt.

THE GUY LUNGED A THIRD TIME.

Sirens chirped, and a police car pulled into sight.

It distracted Josh, and the guy clipped him on the cheek.

"Fuck." That hurt.

"What's going on?" The officer's tone was friendly as he stepped from his car, but his hand hovered near his holster.

Josh held his hands up, shoulder level and palms out. "Good question."

"Let's just move away from each other while we get things sorted, shall we?" The office stepped between them.

Josh complied, and was half-surprised when the pickup driver did the same.

Over the next few minutes, a firetruck ambulance arrived, as well as a couple more cop cars.

An officer and an EMT led Josh in one direction and Pickup Guy in another. The EMT checked Josh for surface injuries, while the officer asked for his version of the story. He'd been driving, the light was green, and someone plowed into him in the intersection.

Pickup Guy told a very different tale. It was easy to hear most of it, due to his volume.

The tow trucks showed up during the conversation. Josh would never drive that Honda again. Thank God for gap insurance, or he'd be paying off a totaled piece of junk for another couple years.

"You look fine on the surface," the EMT said. "You'll want to visit the hospital and get checked out more completely."

"Definitely." If anything was wrong, Josh wasn't letting it wait.

He got the case information from the officer, then called a friend, David, for a ride to the hospital.

At least the day couldn't get much worse.

SYDNEY'S PULSE RACED A MILLION MILES A MINUTE. SHE couldn't believe she'd slept in. She *never* did that. It had been years since she needed an alarm clock, because her brain woke her up first thing in the morning.

But Dylan was so comfortable and sweet and really fucking incredible last night, her over-active brain had shut off for a few hours.

Now he was sitting on the edge of the bed, staring at her with concern in his eyes.

Pity?

No. She wasn't doing that to herself.

"Syd." His voice was kind. "It's okay. Freaking out won't get you down to the vendor floor any faster."

That was disturbingly rational. "But I need to get

showered and changed…" Could she skip all that and just go downstairs? Sweating all day after not washing off a night of sex? Gross.

"So do it." How was he so calm? Because it wasn't his business on the line.

Neither was hers, technically. She could still be downstairs by eight-thirty. She might miss a person or two, but it wasn't the end of the world.

Damn it. Now she was being reasonable, like him.

"How's this?" Dylan said. "Go get ready. I'll do the same, and we'll meet downstairs in fifteen minutes."

"All right." She needed to learn how to do that not-freaking-out thing. "Thank you."

She turned away, but he caught her wrist. He pulled her back to him, wrapped an arm around her waist, and kissed her hard. "I'll see you soon. Promise."

Heat flooded her cheeks, and she couldn't fight her dopey grin. "Okay."

She headed back to her room, her mind working on overtime. She couldn't believe last night happened. Was this a done-and-gone kind of thing? He was sticking around to help her with her booth. He had yet to mislead her, as far as she knew.

If she was going to spend more time with him, she should trust him at least a little at some point. Hell, she'd let him get her off while a room full of strangers watched.

Sydney reached her room and started getting ready.

Last night felt genuine—his words, his actions…

There had been a tiny voice in the back of her head since she met Dylan, that insisted he was making fun of her. Having a silent laugh at the expense of the chubby geek chick. She knew that voice, because it was always there. Most of the time she could ignore it, but when things were going too good, or too badly, it made itself known.

If Dylan's interest in her was a joke, he was an Oscar-quality actor. And if not, she was hooked on him.

Who was she kidding? She was hooked either way.

Would they see each other after the con? Could whatever this was become more? She was willing to push aside some shyness and ask, for a chance like this.

She showered and dressed in record time. One nice thing about running late—it cut out the opportunity to overthink her wardrobe.

She arrived at the vendor hall about the same time as Dylan.

His smile sent delicious tingles racing over her. "Shall we?" he asked.

"Let's."

He wrapped an arm around her waist, as if it were the most natural thing in the world.

What was she doing? She didn't care. This was fun. Delicious. Exciting.

They cut through the people, to get to her booth. A few con-goers were already hanging out, waiting to buy. The vendor next door had kept an eye on the place for her.

Sydney thanked the woman profusely and insisted lunch was on her.

Now, though? It was time to get to work.

The day passed quickly. Because it was Saturday, there was a whole new crowd who'd been working when the con started. It didn't leave a lot of time for chatting, but sales were fantastic.

She found herself reaching for Dylan's hand during lulls, and he always squeezed back with a reassuring smile.

A billion hours later—or ten—the vendor hall closed its doors to attendees.

Dylan slid up behind her and tugged her close. "What are your plans for the night?" His voice vibrated through her back.

Sydney could guess where the conversation was leading. Part of her wanted to opt in for a Round Two of last night. The rest of her was exhausted. "Honestly? Saturday nights are usually *soak my feet, take it easy, and tell myself I only have one more day* kind of nights."

"Don't you love conventions?" Dylan asked.

"So much. But they're draining. I usually need a day or two to sleep and recover after each one."

"After helping you once, I can see why. Are you interested in unwinding with me?"

"Yes." This was her best chance to find out what she needed to know. If she didn't find out now, it would gnaw at her. "But I have to ask you something first."

"Anything."

Of course that was his answer. Because she was trapped in a fairy tale, he was the perfect prince, and she never wanted to wake-up. "Is this going somewhere? You and me?" she asked. "I mean, I'm not asking for long-term commitment, and we don't have to put a definition on it—though if that happened in the future… Rather, is there a future? Do we see each other again after tomorrow? Or is this a one-weekend deal?"

"God, I hope not."

She twisted free from his arms to face him, and studied him with disbelief. Which question was that an answer to?

Dylan laughed. "I'll be more specific. I'd like to see you again. I'm really enjoying spending time with you."

"Yeah?" It was what she'd hoped for, but hearing the words still made her heart flutter.

"Yeah." Dylan nodded. "I don't know what to do, besides be me, to show you I'm sincere. Come up to my room. We'll set alarms on both of our phones and on the hotel clock, and schedule a wake-up call, so we don't oversleep. And if our night is chilling out and nothing more, I'm fine with that."

It was like someone made him in a computer. "Sounds perfect."

They rode the elevator up, and walked to his room.

Dylan unlocked the door and let them in.

Sydney's heart leaped into her throat when she saw someone else was already in there.

Not just someone.

Josh?

"Josh. Hey. Didn't think you'd make it." Dylan sounded like seeing her ex in his room was the most normal thing in the world.

Josh looked past him, to her. "Sydney?"

She worked her jaw up and down, trying to force something, anything from her throat.

What the fuck was her ex-boyfriend doing in her new not-quite-boyfriend's hotel room, and why didn't Dylan look surprised?

Josh struggled to take his eyes off Sydney. Partly because she was one of the last people he expected to see again, but also because she was more stunning than he remembered—perfect curves, and that hint of hesitation in the way she bit her bottom lip.

"Is this why you ignored my texts?" he asked Dylan. He needed something to distract him from the disquieting spike of jealousy.

She was his ex. He didn't have a right to feel jealous.

Sydney met his gaze. "He's helping me with my booth."

Those gorgeous blue eyes weren't any less distracting.

Dylan smirked. "Plus some after-hours extra-curricular activities." He leaned closer to Josh. "I mean sex," he said in a stage whisper.

Sydney ducked her head.

At least there was a little fun to go along with his twinge of envy.

"So… you two know each other." Sydney said it as a statement, rather than a question. "Of course you do. You both work for *Ms. Hunter*."

"I think that's my line." Josh ignored the whisper of venom. Sydney had never gotten along with his mother. "How have you been, Tink?"

"Good."

Dylan held up his hands. "*Tink?* Like, *The* Tink? The girlfriend?"

"Ex," Sydney said.

Josh hated how quickly the correction came, but he didn't blame her.

She took several steps back toward the door. "The room is more occupied that I expected. I should…"

Would she finish the thought? Josh wasn't stupid or blind. He'd seen the way she was looking at Dylan when they walked in. Once upon a time, Josh would have seized this opportunity. A chance to draw Sydney into one of their fantasies, of sharing her. They'd never found a situation she was comfortable with.

Tonight he was the uncomfortable part of that equation.

"I'll leave you two to catch up." Sydney grabbed the door handle.

Dylan strode toward her and loosely grasped her hand. "Don't go."

"It's okay." Her tone was the flat one that meant she was hiding how she really felt. "We were just going to watch movies, anyway. Are you still available tomorrow?"

Dylan stepped closer to her, and Josh clenched his jaw.

"This doesn't change anything. I can keep you company in your room as well as in mine." Dylan's voice was soft.

She shook her head. "I really am exhausted. It's not a big deal. I'll get some sleep and catch up tomorrow."

"If you're sure." Dylan trailed a finger down her arm. "He's my roommate. I see him almost every day. He can wait."

Great. That made Josh feel special.

"It's all right. Stay here. I promise it's not a big deal," Sydney said.

"I'll see you downstairs, tomorrow morning. And everything else we talked about still stands." Dylan pressed his lips to hers, lingering long enough to draw a moan.

When they broke apart, Sydney glanced at Josh. "Catch you around." And then she was gone.

That was super awkward. "Didn't mean to cockblock."

Dylan sat on the edge of one of the beds. "Funny how you say that now, but I didn't hear you offer to leave."

So much for bros before—

That wasn't right.

Dicks before—

Josh didn't like the sound of that one either. "I didn't consider it. My bad."

"As long as you're not going to suggest I stop dating her." Dylan unlaced his shoes, toed them off, and set them aside.

"*Dating?* You've only known her a few days. And no, I'm not going to suggest that."

"Good. Because otherwise, I'd have to say *no* to you, and that might strain our friendship." Tension ran through Dylan's teasing.

Josh needed to back off. He should have anyway. This didn't involve him, and his breakup with Sydney wasn't her fault. Nothing to warn Dylan away from.

Josh was the one who fucked that up.

"That's really Tink?" Dylan's animosity had vanished. "You were right about those hints of naughty she's hiding from the world."

And just like that, the jealousy surged back. Josh had a couple of choices—he could go back to playing the bro card, with, *I used to date her; you can't,* or he could grow up and move on, the way he should have already done.

He didn't care for either solution.

DYLAN HEADED TO SYDNEY'S BOOTH IN THE MORNING with Josh by his side. He'd explained to Josh that he was helping out with Sydney's work all weekend, and they could catch up after the con.

Josh wanted to see the booth and promised to keep his attitude to himself.

Dylan wasn't used to being at odds with Josh. They'd only known each other for a few years, but they got along great. Hell, they'd even explored the *friends with benefits* part of a relationship on several occasions.

When Dylan found out who Sydney was though, a sharp current of possessiveness coiled inside. He didn't know what he had with her, but he wasn't ready to give it up.

They reached Sydney's booth, and she was there and set up for the day. Dylan gave her a *hello* kiss. He didn't see any reason to hold back from how he wanted to act.

"You're selling this? I didn't think they had a distributor," Josh said.

Dylan turned to see him holding one of the C&C boxes.

Sydney snapped off a laugh. "You're kidding, right?"

Dylan added two and two, and got *royally fucked with a side of conflict of interest*. Why didn't he see it sooner? This wasn't someone else's game. It was Sydney's.

"No." Josh shook his head.

Sydney grabbed the box from him and set it neatly back on the stack. "It's *my* game."

Yup. Fuck.

"It's R.H. Pratt's game," Josh said.

"My maternal grandfather. I put his name on the company and the box, for credibility."

People wander the aisles, scoping out the goods for the last day of the con.

"Well, fuck." Dylan expected his career to conflict with his personal life at some point. He hadn't expected it to happen on his first real case.

Sydney's frown deepened, and she looked between them. "Care to share this bad news with me?"

Josh patted Dylan on the shoulder. "Your case. Your girl. Your news."

"I'm one of the lawyers negotiating the distribution deal between R.H. Pratt and the new publisher," Dylan said.

Sydney stepped back, arms crossed. This didn't look good. "You think that might have been important to tell me two days ago?"

Dylan winced. He didn't want to admit what his thought process had been, but he was going to have to. "It didn't occur to me that it was important."

"This game. This one, right here. That you've been selling all weekend." She patted the box. "You didn't figure it was crucial to mention your relationship to it?"

"Well?" Josh was enjoying this too much.

"I—" This was going to sound bad.

Sydney looked at him expectantly. "Yes?"

"I didn't realize it was *your* game. I thought you were working for the guy who created it, and you wouldn't care who he signed contracts with, as long as you still had a job."

Sydney scrubbed her face. "Nice. Wonderful. Unfucking-believable. I don't even want to unpack the assumptions in that statement."

"I can still help you sell today. Our goal is the same—get your game in more people's hands." Dylan had no idea how to make this right. He didn't even know if he should try.

It wasn't that he thought his client would try to screw Sydney over during negotiations, but his job was to get said clients the best deal. He couldn't give them his full representation if he was worried about her on a personal level.

Sydney didn't sleep well last night. Seeing Josh again tugged at something inside she thought was gone.

It should be. It needed to be. And now that she had time to prep herself, she could ignore their past.

Except she was seeing his roommate. Was *dating* the right word? Probably, if they were going to keep seeing each other after the convention.

She didn't think Josh would tell horrible stories about her—maybe she was wrong, but that wasn't like him. She was worried he and Dylan would agree it wasn't cool for a buddy to date his friend's ex.

It shouldn't have kept her up all night, worrying if she'd ever see the guy again who she'd known for all of a weekend, but it did.

When both guys approached her booth and Dylan greeted her as if everything was fine, some of her tension ebbed.

Until Josh dropped the big bomb.

And Dylan added a follow-up blow. Apparently her talking about this being *her* company, *her* game, hadn't been enough of a clue for him.

Because he'd assumed some guy created it.

Okay, so she used initials everywhere, to perpetuate that impression, but…

"Isn't sticking around a form of conflict of interest?" Sydney tried to keep her tone cool. "I don't want you to jeopardize anything by hanging out with the defendant."

"You're not the *defendant.* The goal is that both parties walk away from the negotiating table happy," Dylan said.

She looked past him, to Josh. "Does Ms. Hunter see it that way?" Sydney was certain the woman saw her as the competition even when a contract negotiation wasn't on the table.

Josh held up his hands. "I'm not on the legal team. She booted me to a new case."

Which probably meant the case wasn't significant enough for the boss's son to get his feet wet with it. Josh thought he didn't get any special attention in the firm, but Sydney had seen numerous indicators to the contrary, even pre-law school, when he was an assistant.

"It doesn't matter if I walk away now or in eight hours," Dylan said. "I'm not going to enjoy your company any less. Tomorrow morning, I'll recuse myself and ask someone else to take my place. I'm not a key figure."

And it wasn't a high-profile case. She hesitated to accept. That he'd offered warmed her from the inside out and automatically placed him another rung above Josh, who'd done the opposite when it came up. Several times.

But she also barely knew Dylan, and this was start of his career.

"No you won't." Josh broke in before she could respond. "You're going to woo this client and kick ass on their behalf."

"At least some things never change." This time the bitterness spilled into Sydney's voice. "Go enjoy the con. Both of you." She grabbed Dylan's hand and shook it. Might as well play it cool. "It was nice meeting you. Thanks for the fun. Have a nice life. Good luck with your job."

Dylan gripped tight, keeping her from letting go. "Hang on. He doesn't speak for me. Did you let him speak for you, when you were dating? His answer isn't mine."

She didn't know where to go from here. The distribution offer already had her on edge. She couldn't afford a lawyer for this negotiation. A friend had offered to go over the fine print. Josh wasn't going to point out places for her to be wary. She wished she could trust him for that, but he'd proven repeatedly that the law firm came first.

Dylan might tell her, but that put his job at risk. She wasn't his client.

"Listen." Dylan dropped her hand, but his tone kept her attention. "It doesn't matter if I walk away now. I already know you. I already like you. That conflict doesn't vanish if I abandon you for a few hours of booth work. And there's nothing I can do about it right this second. Let me help you finish out the day, and tomorrow I'll talk to the people in charge about next steps."

"Thank you." Sydney didn't think his talking to the boss would help, but she couldn't turn him down.

Josh's clenched jaw said he disagreed.

That hurt. If Dylan was a new lawyer, he wouldn't have a big impact on a simple contract negotiation. Did Josh hold that much animosity toward her?

DYLAN HAD HOPED THAT WHATEVER BAD FEELINGS remained between Sydney and Josh would take more than two-point-five seconds to emerge.

"Don't go anywhere," he said to Sydney.

She raised an eyebrow. "This is my booth. I'm here the rest of the day."

"Right. Perfect. I'll be back, I promise." He grabbed Josh's arm and yanked him down the aisle. "What the fuck? Seriously."

Josh's scowl deepened. Apparently, that was possible. "This is the start of your career. You spent almost a decade in college to get here. You're going to start off on the wrong foot, for a girl you just met?"

Melodramatic much? "You mean this could be the start of *your* career. But you'll have other ways to get to know the publisher."

"Dylan." Sydney's plaintive tone carried over the morning chatter. "I'm sorry to interrupt…"

He glanced over his shoulder, to see a small crowd had gathered in her booth and she was telling three different people she'd be right with them.

"You're not changing my mind," Dylan said to Josh and turned away. He joined Sydney in the booth. "Who's next?" He called.

He'd expected it to be busier today. Attendance would be at its highest, and people had been saving their money all weekend and would spend today.

But it was different, experiencing the crowds from this side of the vendor table. Sydney's insistence on getting some rest last night made a lot of sense.

At one point, he looked up and realized Josh had stuck around and was helping customers too. He was even talking up the board game.

They kept busy most of the day. The five- and ten-minute lulls were enough for one of them to take a break but didn't leave any time for chatting. Even after the vendor hall closed, attendees dawdled.

Sydney dropped into a chair when the last person was gone. Her face was flushed, but her smile looked etched in place. "Thank you for sticking around. Both of you. If it comes down to it tomorrow morning, I'll pretend I don't know Dylan."

"You'd better not." Possessiveness surged inside Dylan. "Wait. Why just me?" That made it worse.

"Everyone there already knows at least a little of my history with Josh," Sydney said.

Josh shrugged and gave a half nod.

Of course they did. Something about the comment tickled the back of Dylan's mind. He reached for the thought, but it flitted out of his grasp. It would come back if it was important. "I'll recuse myself. It's not going to be an issue."

He expected a protest or at least a growl from Josh, but his roommate stayed impassive.

"When did the two of you meet?" Sydney stood and moved to the closest shelf. "And if you want to help me tear things down, Dylan, it all goes in the same boxes it came from during setup."

Dylan was happy to see this through. He moved to another shelf. He'd spent the day putting together the pieces of when his meeting Josh feel in the *breakup* timeline. It couldn't be a pleasant memory for Josh or Sydney. How much did he want to say?

"I needed a roommate. He was advertising," Josh said. He picked a third shelf and started unloading games into their boxes.

That was about as direct and clean as the answer to that question got.

"So, it was literally right after…" Sydney trailed off.

Josh nodded.

The story Dylan knew was that Josh and Sydney

were going to move in together. She broke up with him after he'd already surrendered his old to live with her, and rather than argue with her over who would stay in the apartment they'd rented together, he let her take it.

"He's a great date, by the way," Josh teased. "The two of you will have fun."

Sydney looked surprised, and Dylan rolled his eyes. "Not like that."

She studied him. "How many ways are there to be someone's date?"

"We were…" What was the best way to phrase this? "Each other's *plus ones* when an uncomfortable situation called for it."

"Ah. If awkward at business meetings is your idea of a good date, I'll be a blast at firm parties." A hint of tension leaked into Sydney's voice. She finished boxing the items on her shelf and moved on to dismantling empty racks. "But I bet the two of you made an adorable couple." Flirting replaced her discomfort.

Dylan smiled. "We turn heads. No question." Something occurred to him. "You know all the deep, dark secrets about Josh that he's never told me."

Josh raised his eyebrows.

"You've met his mother?" Sydney asked.

Considering the woman was Dylan's boss. "Yes…"

"Then he probably has more secrets about me than I can tell you about him."

Odd answer.

"I do know a couple good ones," Josh said before Dylan could question further.

Dylan looked at Sydney. "Do I want to ask?"

"I can tell you a couple of her better fantasies," Josh offered.

Sydney turned bright red. "*No.* No, no, no. Don't you dare."

"You sure? Fifty-fifty chance of living at least one of them out..."

Dylan's curiosity was piqued. Given what he already knew... Memories from the hentai room rushed back. Of Sydney's body, molded to his. The show they'd put on for everyone else. How wet she was. The way she yielded to his touch.

He was definitely curious about what else she had to share.

It was also hers to share. It killed him to say it, but — "I don't want to hear it, unless Sydney wants to tell me."

Fuck, it sucked being a decent person sometimes.

9

Josh didn't know why he was here. He'd joined the mini caravan with Dylan, following Sydney back to her place, to help unload the rest of her merchandise.

Dylan's logic was that, if Josh helped, it would remind him this went beyond conflict of interest, and they could both be guilty at work tomorrow.

Josh caught the glance Dylan sent his say. The implied, *but you leave as soon as the heavy lifting is done.* They'd each driven their own cars, so Josh could leave the new sweethearts alone in peace.

Which didn't help him understand why he'd agreed to join them in the first place.

Because I'm having fun with them.

And because he liked watching Sydney move. And hearing her laugh. And the way she twisted her hair when she was distracted or nervous.

He shook the thoughts aside. Even if she did

decide to spill to Dylan about her two-guys-at-once fantasy, it wasn't going to involve Josh.

They finished stashing her boxes in the second bedroom. She'd stayed in the apartment Josh found with her. They'd gotten a good price on it, so it made sense she stayed here.

The place radiated her personality. Display cases wherever there was space. A futon, and a TV on a cheap stand. Posters, wall scrolls, and merchandise from various fandoms decorated her walls.

He was trying his best not to think about how happy she'd been when she first saw the shower in the master bedroom. Big enough for three people to play in.

Josh wasn't going to be the cockblocking asshole. Not a second time, anyway. He'd let Dylan and Sydney get up to whatever they were going to get up to, and ignore the desire thrumming in his veins. He'd push aside the hedging fantasies of spending one more night stripping Sydney down and making her moan.

He couldn't believe Dylan had surrendered the chance to ask her for more details. The guy must really be smitten.

Dylan wandered toward one of the display cases in the living room. "What are these?"

Josh's thoughts stalled. Dylan was looking at painted figurines for a variety of tabletop games, and she had shelves of them.

"Where are the new ones?" Josh asked.

The look she gave him was difficult to interpret. "Work occupies most of my free time these days. I haven't touched the figurines in a while."

"*You* painted these?" Dylan hovered his hands over the glass, attention fixed on its contents.

Not all of them.

"More than half of them are Josh's," Sydney said.

"I can't believe you kept mine."

She jammed her hands in her pockets. "I couldn't get rid of them. You might be an inconsiderate ass, but you're a talented one."

"Thanks. I think." Josh didn't expect she'd forgiven him, but the reminder was still a painful dig.

Dylan turned back to them. "What class do you play? And don't tell me *it depends*. Everyone has a preference."

"You're not going to just assume I'm the healer?" Sydney asked.

Of course Dylan wouldn't. He knew better. "No, because Josh plays cleric."

"Busted." Sydney laughed. She had relaxed a lot since this morning, and even since they left the convention center. It was nice to see. "Give me two swords and light enough armor to keep me mobile, and send me to the front line."

Dylan looked surprised. "Sounds dangerous."

"She's very agile," Josh assured him.

"Is that a double entendre?"

Sydney stepped closer to Dylan. "If that fills your head with naughty thoughts, then yes."

"I miss those games." What Josh really wanted to say was, *enough with the flirting,* but that was petty. Besides, he didn't actually mind. He thought he would, but Dylan and Sydney looked good together. The one regret Josh had was being on the outside. If he was putting this much thought into the situation, he needed to say his *goodbyes* soon.

He didn't know how much longer he could hold the vivid images at bay, of having Sydney sandwiched between them.

"It wouldn't work now," Sydney said. "We'd make a lousy party."

Right. They were still talking about roleplaying. The not-naked kind. "Why not?" he asked.

"Because your tank would get in my way." Sydney poked Dylan playfully in the chest.

Not the answer Josh expected, but one that made him smile.

"You're the agile one." Dylan grasped her wrist, holding her captive. "You can figure out a way to dance around me with your *two swords*. And I'm flattered you didn't peg me for a bruiser."

Sydney shook her head. "Only when your team is in trouble. Then you'll rain fire down from above. Doesn't matter if it's in your skillset or not."

"Did you ever have a chance to try out the shower?" Josh's question slipped out without his permission. Wow. Way to make things awkward.

Sydney raised her eyebrows. "I use it on pretty much a daily basis."

"This is about *the secret,* isn't it? Do I need to make him leave before I ask again?" Dylan gestured at Josh. "Because I'm trying to behave and not push the issue, but I like knowing secrets. Especially when they're about things that make you moan." He kissed her fingertips.

Sydney fiddled with a loose strand of hair as she looked between Dylan and Josh. "Josh knows. It's not like asking him to leave keeps him from finding out."

SYDNEY WAS TRYING TO IGNORE HER BODY'S REACTION TO Josh, and failing. Not that she was giving up on Dylan. Holy wow, she wasn't walking away from a guy like that. But was there really any harm in putting the information out there, to see how Dylan reacted?

It wasn't like she wanted Josh back. He was attractive. He was fun. And he still had the same habits that drove them apart. But this didn't have to involve him.

"We got the apartment with the extra-big shower because I like shower sex," Sydney confessed.

Dylan's hungry smile sent happy shivers racing down her spine. "So let's kick him out, and we'll go get clean."

Josh gave her a pointed look. "And?"

"And it's big enough for more than two people. For three, actually. Because I think it would be fun"—hot, sexy, incredible—"to be with two guys at the same time." *Please don't let this confession backfire.* It wasn't as though she was saying she wanted to fuck her ex-boyfriend.

She'd probably do it. But not at the cost of pushing Dylan away.

Dylan searched her face. "The shower implies it was more than just a passing fancy."

"We'd started to look for a third before we broke up," Josh said.

Dylan glanced at him. "You never told me that."

What kind of relationship did they have, that Josh would share something like this with Dylan?

Josh sighed. "I didn't have the same interest in it without Sydney."

The revelation clenched around her heart. She didn't expect that kind of reaction—from herself or from him.

Josh looked at her. "I still like the idea. But it was your fantasy."

What was she supposed to say? It hurt to leave Josh, but she'd convinced herself he walked away unscathed. At least part of her knew that wasn't true, but admitting he was affected as well cut deep. She didn't expect her own reaction.

"I kind of feel like I should have stayed out of this," Dylan said. "I'm not sure if I regret pushing for an answer."

Please, please don't let this turn him off or push him away. "Would you still feel uncertain if the fantasy wasn't attached to Josh?" Because it wasn't. She needed to say that aloud. The second guy, feeling her up from behind while Dylan kissed her passionately, didn't have a face.

"You don't want my answer." Dylan's tone had shifted to something she couldn't decipher. It wasn't flat or angry or unhappy.

Sydney frowned. This was falling apart fast. What did she expect? New boyfriend plus ex-boyfriend equaled disaster. But she didn't expect this would be the impetus. "I do. Want your answer, that is."

Dylan raised her hand to kiss her palm. It was such a tender, sweet gesture. It didn't comfort her.

"It makes it better, not worse, that Josh is part of it." Dylan's lips tickled her skin as he spoke.

"Oh." Way to sound intelligent. She should be bothered by his admission, but heat raced over her skin, and the images dancing in her thoughts solidified.

Dylan dropped her hand and traced her bottom lip with his finger. "Don't get me wrong. I don't like the idea of sharing you, in general. That's selfish of me, since we haven't talked about exclusivity, but there you have it."

"But?" Her voice cracked on the word. She needed to open a window. Turn on the air. Stick her head in the freezer.

"But in the hentai room—"

"The *what*?" Josh asked.

It was going to be a long night if this conversation didn't find a conclusion.

Dylan kept his attention on her. "That was hot."

"It really was." And with the memory added on top of desire, Sydney had to squeeze her thighs together, to mute the pulse between her legs.

Josh cleared his throat. "Details?"

Sydney had questions for Dylan. "Why does he matter? Why does he make the fantasy better?"

"Because he *does* matter to me," Dylan said. "I trust him. I like him. He's a fun date and a good lay."

She couldn't argue those last few words. She'd run out of reasons why this was a bad idea, beyond *ex-boyfriend*. She looked at Josh. "We got ourselves invited to a party the first night of the con. It turned out to be a bunch of people, watching anime porn and getting off to it."

"And you joined them." Was that jealousy in Josh's voice?

Sydney shrugged.

"I helped her put on a show," Dylan offered.

Josh stared at her, desire heavy in his eyes. *Fuck,* she missed that look.

She turned back to Dylan. "There's no universe where this seems like a smart idea. But it's tempting." What was she saying? *Shut up.*

She didn't want to listen to that voice, though.

Dylan searched her face. "It is, isn't it?"

"I'm offering fantasy fulfillment. One night only. I'll leave the two of you be, after," Josh said.

Fucking hell. Sydney was teetering on a sharp edge. Falling in one direction was safety and disappointment and boredom. And in the other direction was impulsive stupidity, with a high probability of a couple amazing orgasms and some fantastic memories.

Dylan cupped her cheeks, holding her gaze. "Are you okay with this?"

"I think that's supposed to be my question to you." Her throat was dry. She licked her lips and swallowed, but it didn't help.

"You have to tell me you're all right with all three of us together. Or I'll kick Josh out now. I'll leave too, if you want."

She didn't want either one of them to leave. Her answer froze in her throat. This was one more night with Josh, no strings, and living out one of her biggest fantasies with Dylan. She couldn't turn that down. "You should both stay."

Dylan crushed his mouth to hers, and her pulse soared. All of her doubt evaporated. He licked along her bottom lip, and she let his tongue in, to dance with hers.

A second pair of hands rested on her hips, and her heart slammed into her rib cage. And then Josh's lips were on the back of her neck, gliding up to the hollow behind her ear. The spot he knew drove her wild.

Yeah, this was a terrible fucking idea. And Sydney was going to enjoy every minute of it.

Dylan liked this whole threesome idea as a general concept—Sydney plus one more—but Josh was shattered by the breakup when Dylan met him, and it probably wasn't any easier on Sydney.

Sydney and Josh were adults. If they were okay with this, it wasn't Dylan's place to tell them they were wrong.

Besides, he liked Sydney's fantasies so far, he wasn't going to discourage them. Desires like this were a horrible thing to suppress.

He dragged his mouth down her neck and nudged aside her shirt collar.

"No." Her protest was weak. She rested a hand on his chest but didn't push him away.

He looked up to meet her gaze. Not the best time for second thoughts, but certainly her right. "What's wrong?" he asked. It was impossible to ignore the way Josh still gripped her hips.

"Nothing. I mean, not with what you're doing. But I'm all sweaty and gross from the convention. You may not want to be kissing all over me like this."

That was it? Fortunately, there was a solution in place. "Do you want to get in the shower, fully clothed?"

Sydney shook her head.

"Then the clothes have to come off." Dylan tugged her shirt over her head. "And it's up to me if I mind a little sweat or not." He lowered his mouth to her neck and kissed along the long curve while he dragged his palms up her sides.

Her bra fell away. In the wave of kissing and groping, his touch collided with Josh's several times. Another reason for Dylan to enjoy this. He brought his mouth back to Sydney's, to swallow her moans.

Josh cupped her breasts, and Dylan dragged his thumbs across her nipples. She whimpered and pressed into Dylan's touch.

The heat and desire flooding him set his thoughts ablaze. This didn't seem like one of those things people just fell into, but here he was… and *fuck,* he liked the potential rolling out in front of them.

He bit Sydney's bottom lip and dove deeper into the kiss. Each time he rolled her nipples between his fingers, pinched or pulled, she made another delicious sound and molded to his touch in a new way.

Josh's hands had traveled lower, to undo her jeans

and tease along her waist. She squirmed her hips against the contact, and Dylan wasn't complaining about either of them brushing or grinding against him in the process.

Sydney broke the kiss with a breathless gasp and stepped away from them. She searched Dylan's face, mischief dancing behind her eyes. That playful look alone was enough to undo him.

"I want to watch the two of you strip." Her request was a combination of shy and bold that shouldn't work together. She owned it, though.

He exchanged a glance with Josh, who shrugged. "I'm not really a dancer," Josh said.

"Which I know is a lie. But I'm not expecting *Magic Mike* choreography. I do want to see some asses wiggling." Sydney fixed her attention on Dylan.

He kicked his shoes aside. "Do we get music?"

"I can hum the Jeopardy theme, but that might be a mood killer," Sydney teased.

Dylan was always up for a challenge. He swayed his hips and slid his hands up his sides then back down, to tug up the bottom of his shirt. The way Sydney watched him—eyes wide, bottom lip caught between her teeth—made him harder than he thought possible and had his pulse hammering in his ears.

Her gaze drifted to Josh every few seconds. Dylan expected jealousy, but he was stealing the occasional look as well.

Josh was also going to make a show of this. He turned with his back to her. before stripping off his T-shirt, letting the stretch of his arms elongate his torso, and enjoying the heat of her attention flowing over him.

Dylan undid his jeans and let them drop low on his hips. The whistle he received in return was worth it. He liked to watch, but he'd never considered the thrill of being the one on display. It was exhilarating. As he spun back to face Sydney, he stole another glance at Josh, who was in a similar state of undress.

Wiry cords of muscle rippled under Josh's skin, showing off the athletic frame his clothes usually hid.

Dylan met Sydney's gaze again and pushed his jeans to the floor.

She twisted her mouth and raised an eyebrow, but it didn't hide her smirk. "Take it *all* off."

"You wanted a show." Dylan hooked his thumbs in the elastic of his boxers, inching them lower as he moved closer to her.

"I did. And I'm liking what I'm seeing." She covered his hands and coaxed them down. "But I want to touch, too." She pushed the rest of his clothes to the ground, and his cock sprang free. When she gripped his shaft, a low groan tore from his throat.

He knotted his fingers in her hair and claimed her mouth. His erection dug into her belly. She molded to him. And there was that third set of hands in there, Josh's, cupping her breasts as he pressed into her back.

"If you're not careful, we won't make it to the shower." Josh's warning was a low growl.

"He's got a good point." Dylan murmured against Sydney's lips.

She stepped from their grasp, and took them both by the hand. "I guess we'd better move, then."

FAMILIAR TOUCHES.

New ones.

More hands on her bare skin than there should be.

Sydney wanted to memorize every tantalizing brush of skin on skin.

Hot water poured over the three of them. Sydney was more scalded by Josh's open-mouth kisses up her spine and the way Dylan sucked along her shoulder hard enough to leave his mark.

She couldn't ignore Josh. Which made sense—he was drawing soapy trail along the inside of her thigh—but there was more to it. She liked this excuse to feel him again.

She was just as focused on Dylan—he glide of his hands along her torso, as he washed her clean and followed behind with hungry kisses. She gripped his cock loosely. He jerked against her hand each time she squeezed, spiking her desire.

Josh's erection dug into one ass cheek. A reminder of how good it felt when he was inside her. Each grip and grope made the need between her legs throb more insistently.

Dylan extracted the portable shower head from its

socket. "This looks like fun. Not that a sweet girl like you would know about that." His tone was playful.

"It is fun. And I do know." Sydney was enjoying how easy things were with him. "A sweet girl has to entertain herself when there's no one around to help."

"Sweet and innocent?" Josh's question vibrated against her shoulder. He drew his fingers up the inside of her thigh, to tease along her slit.

She gasped. "One-hundred percent innocent."

Dylan flicked his thumb over the switch on the shower head, changing it to a massage setting. "And naive?"

"Let's not get carried away…" Her reply faded into a moan when Dylan lowered the nozzle and the water pounded her skin.

He parted her lower lips and moved the shower head forward. The stream hammered against her clit, stealing her breath.

Dylan claimed her mouth, holding the nozzle in place while he drank her whimpers.

Josh slipped two fingers inside her, and she arched her back, not sure which way to lean to feel *everything*.

Waves of pleasure rocked her body. Her thoughts swam on the crest as the men coaxed her closer to the edge of orgasm. Josh pumped, and Dylan didn't let up.

She came hard, screaming into the kiss and grinding against Josh's hand until it was too much. Her body shuddered away from the shower head, but she didn't want to let go of Dylan. Being pressed between the men was the one thing making it possible for her wobbly legs to hold her upright.

"*Fuck*, I missed making you come." Josh's whisper caressed her ear, so soft it was more of a suggestion than a sound. Did Dylan hear that? The words fluttered in her belly and clenched like a fist around her heart at the same time.

She shook aside the nagging regret. She wasn't going to second-guess her past because of a great orgasm.

Dylan replaced the shower head in its dock, then licked a path down her chest, to tease a nipple with his tongue. "All clean. I can nibble on whatever I want." He scraped his teeth over the sensitive nub.

She groaned and pushed into his mouth. "Okay." Her grasp of complex words had evaporated.

"Here's the thing…" Josh bit her shoulder, and she groaned. "This is a lot of fun, but I'm not sure the mechanics of actual sex are going to work in here."

He was right. There was plenty of room for three people, and a delicious hum still rolled over her skin from her climax, but she didn't know how anything complex could take place in this space. "What did you have in mind?"

"We dry off enough to not drip on the carpet, and move this into the bedroom," Josh said.

"I guess." Sydney let out an exaggerated huff.

Dylan shut off the water, then grasped her fingers and helped her step from the shower.

Being patted dry with a big fluffy towel was fun,

but she was looking for a different kind of closure. One that involved feeling Dylan's thick cock stretching her out again.

He looked over her shoulder. "Condoms?"

"Don't have any," Josh said.

A twinge of something negative pinged inside Sydney, because she wasn't surprised he wasn't carrying protection. Josh was always Josh's priority. She ignored it.

"I do. In my wallet." Dylan kissed her fingertips. They made their way to the bedroom, with a quick detour for protection.

He stopped with his back to the bed, facing her. She couldn't help but notice he kept positioning her so she was looking at him, not Josh.

Not that Sydney minded. This was an easier way to keep things from getting more complicated.

So I'm just using Josh for the sex?

That was what they'd agreed on.

"What do you want?" Dylan asked. "Your fantasy. You drive."

Sydney liked the sound of that. "Does that mean I get to owe you a fantasy in return?"

"I have a feeling there will be a lot of give on that front. For both of us." He smirked.

She liked that even more. "I want you inside me. Both of you." She and Josh'd had anal sex several times, so she knew what to expect.

He seemed to remember too, since he didn't hesitate to grab the lube from the top drawer of her dresser.

Dylan settled on the bed and rolled on a condom. He crooked his finger and gestured for her to come closer. "I like the idea of watching you ride me. You make the most gorgeous faces when you get caught up in the moment."

A fresh wave of heat spread through her. She climbed up his legs and hovered over his length.

Dylan *tsk*ed and gripped her hip with one hand. "A guy can only take so much teasing." He fisted his shaft and thrust his hips up, plunging inside her.

His groan mingled with hers, as he filled her up and spread her open. So much better than fingers.

She rocked against him, letting him set a slow but steady pace.

Josh glided his fingers, slick with lube, along her ass. He teased her second hole. This was good. This was better than good, and it was just a hint.

Dylan paused, and Josh nudged her with the head of his cock.

Her breath hitched with anticipation.

Josh kissed the edge of her ear. "You okay?"

She nodded. A little sensory-overloaded maybe, but okay.

He eased in, pausing with every inch, to let her adjust and relax. The penetration seemed to take forever, and then he was inside her, chest pressed to her back.

It was different and incredible, being stretched out

this way. With both men thrusting. Building up to a decent rhythm again.

The friction, the contact, being sandwiched between them—it short-circuited her thoughts. Dylan glided his hands up her stomach, to caress her breasts, drawing her further into the lovely clouds flitting around her thoughts.

Josh reached around to find her clit. Her body jerked away instinctively, but she leaned back in. His stroke was gentle and coaxing.

The sum of every touch and groan built in her veins, scorching her with a surging climax.

Josh still knew exactly which spot to hit, both inside and out, and Dylan read her cues without pause. She fell into orgasm, tumbling through the pleasure overload.

The familiar grunts, punctuated with long pauses, told her Josh was close. The way Dylan's face scrunched up said he was too. Thrusting became frantic pounding as they came.

As the frenzied pace slowed, then stopped, she slipped back from the edge. But part of her lingered in the haze. She rested her head on Dylan's chest and listened to the heavy thrum of his heartbeat as they caught their breath.

Josh slipped out of her, and a moment later, he collapsed next to them on the bed.

She rolled off Dylan but was reluctant to let go of him. He stripped off his condom and settled back next to her, arm around her waist.

"Everything you dreamed of?" He nuzzled her neck.

"The reality was much better."

She wanted to lie there all night, wrapped up between them, enjoying the afterglow.

Doubt weaseled back in. A question she'd been trying to ignore all night. The one that mocked her for months after she broke up with Josh. Did she overreact back then?

She was just starting things up with Dylan, and there was no way she'd jeopardize a chance with a guy this great.

Why do I have to choose?

Because that was the way the world worked.

"We should go." Josh's voice was quiet but hard, leaving no room for argument.

Dylan rested his forehead against Sydney's shoulder. "He's probably right. We have to work in the morning, and you have a meeting."

Ugh. That.

"Don't forget." Josh met her gaze. "Tomorrow you two don't know each other."

Ice flowed through her veins, and she clenched her jaw. There it was. That distinctly clear reminder of who Josh actually was.

"Don't listen to him," Dylan said. "I'll set him straight at home."

The reassurance didn't settle the churning in her gut.

11

Josh was grateful to be making the drive home alone. It meant he could crank the radio and sing along, rather than listening to his own thoughts.

The last thing he wanted to do was dwell on what a first-class ass he was as they left Sydney's place.

Second-to-last was to remember the past.

Apparently the music wasn't drowning out anything.

Why did he say anything about work? What the fuck was wrong with him?

He didn't want admit the reality. Being with Sydney reminded him how much he enjoyed her company. He missed the sex, sure; she was fun, sexy, and delicious in bed. But he missed *her* more.

Sydney and Dylan clicked. It was easy to see that. They almost radiated sparks. Josh wasn't doing a great job of ignoring the part of him that seethed with jealousy at seeing them together.

Josh wasn't going to act on it, though. Tonight was fun. A one-off. He'd keep his distance. That was the one upside to his comment as he was leaving—it served to push him further away.

When he got home, he'd tell Dylan he didn't mean it and ask him to pass Josh's apologies along to Sydney. Not doing it himself would ring with insincerity. And Josh would suck it up and move on.

A fist clenched around his heart at the idea, and his mind decided now was a great time to traipse into his past.

The guy working the register at the comic shop shook his head. "You can't do that. In the two-point-five ruleset— "

"The secret we should never let the gamemasters know is that they don't need any rules." The woman talking to him was curvy, cute, and irritated. "Go ahead. Ask me who said it."

Josh paused a few feet back, to watch the conversation unfold.

Comic-store Guy pushed his glasses up on his nose. "No one said it. It's an unverified quote frequently attributed to Gary Gygax, with no verifiable source."

"Convenient, since that proves your point. How many unverified quotes do you spit out on a daily basis?" The woman crossed her arms, accentuating her breasts. The instant Comic-store Guy's gaze dropped, she shoved her

hands in her pockets instead. "The point is, if you're not making the game your own, what's the point in playing?"

"You have to play the way the original creators intended."

Josh understood why the woman was annoyed. He stepped forward, to tell the hack to shut the fuck up.

"The original creators"—snideness dripped from the woman's voice—"intended people be creative with the game. If I want to say that werewolves can be killed by—"

"Everyone knows werewolves can only be killed with silver bullets." Comic-store Guy talked over her. He looked at Josh. "Am I right?"

Josh shook his head. "No. You're so very wrong. Shut up."

"Excuse me?" Comic-store Guy's retort came out weakly.

Half a smile flickered on the woman's face, like she was trying to hide her amusement.

Josh winked at her and turned to the guy. "I said, shut the fuck up. I'd like to hear what the lady has to say."

"Because you like her tits?" Comic-store Guy asked.

Josh's hand shot out lightning fast—his aikido training helped with the reflex—and he grabbed Comic-store Guy's shirt collar. He tugged him forward, half-bent over the glass display cabinet. "Because she makes more sense than you. Because she's obviously smarter." Josh let him go and wiped his hand on his jeans. "And because she doesn't have Cheeto dust or Doritos, or whatever the hell that is—dripped down the front of her shirt. I'd say apologize, *but you wouldn't mean it."*

"Fuckin' beta boy fag.'

Josh took a single step forward, and Comic-store Guy took several back.

Josh tossed his comics on the counter. "On second thought, I'll get these on Amazon." He strolled from the store, fury seething white hot under his skin.

When he stepped outside, he realized the woman was next to him.

"Thanks," she said. "Even if you didn't mean it, thank you."

"I absolutely meant it. Josh." He extended his hand.

Her grip was firm, and her skin soft and tantalizing. "Sydney."

"I'd love to hear about alternate rule sets. Can I buy you coffee?"

She ducked her head.

*"What's wrong?" he asked. "*No *is fine."*

Sydney twisted a strand of hair around her ear. "I'm just trying to figure out if coffee *is a euphemism." Her clipped tone implied she'd rather it wasn't. At least right now.*

"It's not." Josh was sincere. "I really do want to hear more. If you want to give me your number when we go our separate ways, that's up to you."

The ache in his chest snapped him back to the present. He'd thought he was over Sydney, but spending the day with her brought it all rushing back.

It didn't matter. Those were whispers of the past. He'd move on, like last time.

When Josh got home, Dylan's car was already in its spot.

In the apartment, Dylan's bedroom door was shut. There was a note scrawled on the whiteboard on the fridge:

You know how I feel. Conversation over.

That settled that. Dylan would do things his way, even if it meant fucking up his career.

And Josh would keep repeating that the matter was closed, until he believed it.

DYLAN SLEPT THROUGH HIS ALARM AND WAS RUSHED TO get to work. It turned out working a convention all weekend, instead of just enjoying it at his own pace, was exhausting.

He was pretty happy with the way everything ended, too. Minus that one dark spot he called his roommate.

Josh was already on his way out when Dylan stumbled into the kitchen for coffee. Josh's, "Tried to wake you up. Glad you figured out consciousness. Tell Sydney I'm sorry," was halfhearted at best.

Dylan brushed it aside and finished getting ready.

An hour later, he sat across from Ms. Hunter, explaining that he wouldn't have pursued the creator if he realized her association with this account, but he had, and now he needed to recuse himself.

When he finished, she stared back impassively.

One day, he was going to learn how she did that. It made her intimidating in a court room... and in an apartment at eight on a Saturday morning, when she was asking Josh in an eerily calm voice why there were takeout bags and beer cans everywhere.

In their defense, it had been finals week, and nothing was getting done except eating, studying, and test taking.

"I appreciate your honesty and professionalism." Her tone was kind but cool. "It's going to serve you well. For today, go ahead and sit in the meeting. You're in there to listen, not advise. After today, you can still be involved behind the scenes, but you won't meet with Sydney again. I trust you to not discuss the contract with her outside of work."

That was kind of permissive. Not that Dylan wanted to argue the best of both worlds scenario, but he had to cover his bases and his ass. "If there's something in the contract that's a threat to Sydney, I won't be able to not tell her."

"I wouldn't expect otherwise, regardless of the client. Have you seen anything that makes you hesitate? If so, I'd also like to know."

He hadn't. There was no language that stole her intellectual property or would take the game from her in any way. The biggest liberty they were taking was the right to edit the game manual, according to their grammar standards. "Her game is worth more."

"Noted, and not our decision. The client offers what they feel is appropriate. It's not your place to push her to ask for more, though I'd understand if you reminded her negotiation is expected when it comes to price."

Okay, well that went far better than his best case scenario. A thought tickled the back of his mind, and he struggled to grasp it. It flitted away. "All right."

"Wonderful. The meeting is in a few minutes. Is there anything else?"

"No. Thank you." He stood.

He was halfway to her office door, when the thought rushed back in. He looked at her again.

"Is there something else?" Ms. Hunter asked.

"You knew who I was talking about. Sydney's name is hidden from all the documents, and I didn't tell you she was who I'm seeing."

"I've done my research."

Which he expected and should have thought of earlier. "She's the reason you pulled Josh from the case. Why is it a conflict of interest for him and not me?"

Laurie Hunter gave him a thin-lipped smile that implied he'd crossed that line between employee and son's best friend, and he needed to step back. "You're reading too much into the situation. Best of luck today."

"Thanks." He'd push for more later, when he wasn't pressed for time.

It was a tiny observation, but it wouldn't leave Dylan alone. Did Ms. Hunter go out of her way to keep Sydney and Josh apart? Why was that necessary? Even if Dylan weren't dating Sydney, it seemed likely her name would come up in conversation at home.

Maybe Dylan *was* reading too much into it.

He grabbed his notebook and paperwork from his office, and joined Aaron Jorgenson and two client representatives in a conference room.

The other three looked up when Dylan entered, and then the editor turned to Aaron. "That's fine. If it's what you describe, I don't see an issue with it."

"Your appointment is here," the receptionist's voice came from behind Dylan, catching him off guard.

He'd have to ask Aaron for details after the meeting.

Aaron stood. "I'll go greet her, make introductions, and we can get started."

Dylan took a seat, a jumble of thoughts racing in his head. Something about this situation was off. He wasn't used to this type of doubt.

Aaron returned a moment later, with Sydney by his side. She was dressed in a simple black pantsuit that was professional and revealed another stunning side of her.

When she saw him, her eyes grew wide, but a tiny smile quickly replaced her surprise. Her shoulders seemed to relax a little.

Aaron introduced her to everyone, finishing with, "And I believe you already know Dylan."

News traveled fast.

Sydney nodded. "It's nice to meet you all."

Aaron gestured to a chair, waited for Sydney to sit, and took his own seat. "Will your attorney be joining us?"

"No. I'm representing myself." Sydney sat like someone had jammed a rod down her spine.

Dylan had known that would be her answer, but the apprehension racing under his skin didn't like it. Who did he know from law school who owed him a favor? Something he could call in for a few free hours of consulting for Sydney. An extra set of eyes, to look over the contract with her.

He'd told Laurie the truth, that he didn't see any issues with the contract, but his concern wasn't evaporating.

"Thank you for coming into the office today." Aaron launched into a smooth, friendly greeting. "I feel like it's better to do these types of meetings in person whenever possible. It lets everyone look each other in the eye, and helps all parties feel better about the process."

"It's not a problem, and I'm looking forward to it." Sydney was cool and collected. Her tension hovered under the surface. He saw it in the tight lines around her eyes, but she hid it well.

Dylan was impressed. And a bit turned on. This was another side of her he liked.

The group went through the contract, with Aaron giving an overview of each section. It was all boilerplate language. The same information Dylan read in preparation.

He still followed along on the copy on his tablet, making notes whenever Aaron used a phrase or definition that Dylan thought was important.

They reached the *Rights* section of the contract. Aaron read a number, but the information that followed didn't match what was in Dylan's document.

Dylan tried to be subtle about scrolling up and down in his file, to see what he'd missed. Why was he out of sync?

"Is there an issue?" Aaron's sharp question drew Dylan's attention from his tablet.

I have the wrong document. Dylan kept the reply to himself. That wasn't the kind of thing to admit in front of the client. "I'm fine. Please continue."

Within a few seconds, he'd located the portion Aaron was reading, but Dylan's copy was numbered differently.

The rest of the meeting continued without a hitch. Sydney asked a few basic questions—Dylan was impressed with the things she honed in on—and was on her way.

He wanted to run after her and give her a goodbye kiss. This didn't seem like the time to push the limits of his employer's leniency, though.

Instead, he headed back to his office, to pull the most recent contract from the file repository on the network.

As he flipped through the official copy, the concern hovering under his skin grew. It was identical to the file Dylan had, and that made it different than the one Aaron had read from.

He fired a quick email off to Aaron, asking about the discrepancy. He didn't have to wait long for a reply.

You're remembering the meeting wrong. Nothing is out of sync. It may be a good thing you're sitting the rest of this case out, if your girlfriend had you that distracted.

Dylan clenched his jaw. He knew what he'd heard. Confronting Aaron or taking things up the ladder hadn't done him any good in the past, since Aaron was fucking Laurie.

But this had the potential to fuck Sydney in a completely different way. Dylan needed to get a hold of the correct contract.

Or was he blowing this up into something it wasn't? Aaron wouldn't pull a bait and switch with a contract. He was an incompetent asshole, but he wasn't willingly performing ethics violations.

Sydney felt like she was watching the contract discussion from a hamster wheel. One someone else was spinning, and she couldn't figure out how to stop. She was used to representing herself in business meetings, when speaking with banks, and in a variety of other situations.

This was a new experience for her, and she hadn't expected to feel so tiny and isolated.

Having Dylan in the room helped a little, except that she didn't know why he was still there, and she didn't dare do anything that might cause him problems with his job.

So she smiled, nodded, and said *goodbye* when it was all over, and walked out the door.

When she reached her car, she sank into the driver's seat and let out a long sigh. Her stomach was tied in knots, and the muscles in her neck weren't doing much better.

The buzz of her phone startled her. She fumbled in her purse and fished it out.

Seeing Dylan's name chased away some of the butterflies, and she smiled.

You did awesome. I'll explain everything after work if you're free.

She was still getting used to him wanting to see her. The weekend hadn't been a dream after all. Her smile grew. *I am.*

Good. Before then, you're going to get a call from Liam. He's a friend from school, and he'll help you with the contract, free of charge. Talk to him. Have him give everything a once over.

More of her tension seeped away. *I will. Thank you. And I owe you.*

I'm sure we can think of a way you can make it up to me ;)

Heat raced over her skin at the subtle innuendo. She could think of a lot of things she'd do to thank Dylan. Some of them involved her being on her knees, and others included straddling his legs…

She squeezed her thighs together at the sharp pulse of need. Fantasy needed to wait until later. At least until she left the parking garage.

Twenty minutes later, she was home. The morning after a convention was usually unwind-and-decompress time. The meeting took that away from her, but she could make it up now. Shed the professional clothes. Spend a little time with her vibrator and memories of last night.

What was up with her? A weekend of getting laid, and now she couldn't get enough?

Not *just* getting laid. It was really good sex.

Tomorrow you two don't know each other.

Josh's sharp voice echoed in her memories, and anger surged inside. Mood. Killed.

She draped her nice clothes over the back of a chair in her bedroom, pulled on something more comfortable, and collapsed on her bed. The ceiling didn't have any more answers about what was wrong with Josh than she'd found anywhere else.

Her thoughts raced around in circles, chasing the reality of fantasy fulfillment, both in the bedroom and with her board game.

Why were both so complicated?

Sydney needed to step outside of her own head. She grabbed her phone and dialed her best friend.

"Hey." Kathryn's greeting was cheerful. "Perfect timing. I just finished a class." Kathryn taught marital arts. She was at least as good as Josh. "How was the con? What did I miss? Did you get laid?"

She asked that every time. She'd met her boyfriends at a convention, and kept insisting that, if she could do it, so could Sydney.

"Yes." Sydney couldn't fight her smirk.

There was a pause, and then, "*Ha*. I told you so. What's he like? Is he sexy? Of course he is. Did you use him and toss him away, or give in and give him your number?"

This was making Sydney feel better. "He has my

number, but I made him beg for it just a little," she joked. "And he's got this roommate..." No. *Fuck.* Why did she say that?

"Ooh. Did you...? I'm guessing, if you mentioned it... How was it?"

"It was good. Incredible." Sydney didn't want to share details. Those were hers. "But it was only a one-time thing. With the roommate, that is."

"You never know." Kathryn's tone was playful. "But either way, at least you had a blast. So, give me details. What are their names?"

The answer stuck in Sydney's throat. When Kathryn met Dylan, the truth was going to come out. And it wasn't like Sydney'd gone back to Josh, so this wasn't a big deal.

"Why are you hesitating?" Kathryn asked.

Busted. "Mr. Has-My-Number is Dylan. His roommate is Josh."

Kathryn sucked in a sharp breath through her teeth, making Sydney wince.

"The name is a coincidence?" Kathryn's cheer had wilted.

Sydney pushed back a wave of defensiveness. Her friend was looking out for her. "No. It was him... And I know, but it was just once, and I didn't know Dylan knew him at first."

"I'm not saying anything." Kathryn's cautious tone implied plenty. "Because you *do* know. Okay, I'm going to say something. If Josh treats you the same way again, I'm grinding his balls into the dirt. I don't care what kind of black belt he has, or if I'm allowed to hit below it; I will."

"It won't happen again. No plans of that at all." Especially with the note he left things on.

A knock filtered in from the front door, and Sydney frowned. "There's someone here. Talk to you soon?"

"Always. But Syd… Please be careful with him."

"Always." Sydney's assurance came out too bright. She disconnected and went to answer the door. When she peered through the peephole, she didn't recognize the man on the other side.

Keeping the security chain in place, she opened the door a crack. "May I help you?"

"I have court papers for Sydney Brimhall." He held up several pieces of paper clipped together, showing her the court markings up top.

Was this the contract from this morning? She already had a copy of that. "Hang on a sec." She closed the door enough to unlatch it, then opened it wider.

He shoved the document at her. "Here. Phone number for questions is on the top. Contact the court or your attorney if you need. Have a nice day." He was walking away before he finished talking.

Not the friendliest guy. Then again, if it was his job to tell people the courts wanted to talk to them, he probably got yelled at a lot.

She leaned against her apartment doorframe, to flip through the paperwork. The *Cease and Desist* on the front page brought back her earlier tension. The *Patent Infringement* a little lower down made bile rise in her throat. What the hell was this?

"Tink? What's wrong?" Josh's voice startled her, and she looked up to find him standing in front of her, watching her with concern.

She should have stepped inside and closed her door.

The sound of his voice sent goosebumps racing over her skin, and at the same time was like nails on a chalkboard. Damn her body for the former. She wasn't in the mood for whatever he wanted. "Did you come by to insult, threaten, or belittle me a little more? Needed to do it in person?"

He raised an eyebrow. "I'm here to apologize. I was going to ask Dylan to intercede on my behalf, but you deserve better than hearing it from a messenger."

That was almost insightful and considerate of him. It didn't make up for the past, recent or longer ago. "Great. Good for you. See you around."

"Tell me what's wrong?"

Why did he care? Besides, she didn't need Josh's help. Dylan said Liam would call her. She could slip in a question about this at the same time. "Nah. I'm good."

"What is this?" Josh angled his body so his shoulder rested against hers, and he could see what was in her had. "Cease and Desist?"

She yanked the document and her arm away. Heat seared her skin where he'd touched. "Nothing for you to worry about. I'm going to discuss it with my attorney."

"You suddenly have a lawyer?"

"Dylan hooked me up with Liam."

Josh clenched his jaw, and his expression almost said *of course he did.*

She liked having news that bothered him but was none of his business. But that didn't erase her worry about the notice she held.

"Tink, you don't have to forgive me. I was a superior ass last night. But let me help you with this?" Concern and sincerity lined his voice. The use of her nickname didn't hurt either.

"This is technically company related. Are you even allowed to talk to me?" She wasn't letting him off the hook.

"If it's not related to your contract, I don't see how telling me could hurt."

She saw a lot of ways it could hurt, but the gnawing pit in her gut wanted her to deal with the issue. If nothing else, he could offer a second opinion. "It's indirectly related to the contract." Since it challenged her ownership of the property. Why was she still talking to him? Because he almost sounded sincere when he apologized, and because she needed answers.

She was going to cave anyway, if he kept asking. Might as well get it over with. She stepped aside. "I'm not saying things are good between us. They're not. But… please take a look?" She handed him the notice.

Josh lingered in the entryway. He scanned the paperwork quietly for a few minutes, then handed it back. "You're being trolled."

"What? Why? How?"

"Patent troll. And in this case, their claim is beyond ludicrous. It's for any board game using characters of a mythological origin."

She knew the term. Patent trolls were entities who filed broad patents, then used them to demand money from anyone who created a product that fell within their sweeping definition. "Do I pay them, then?" That was typically the result. Cheaper to pay them to go away, than to fight them.

"You take them to court." Josh didn't hesitate.

There was no way she could afford that. "I saw that episode of *Silicon Valley*. Once I pay attorney fees, I'll have been better off just writing these guys a check."

"Dylan will help you. I'll help you. I'll tell you exactly what paperwork to fill out, what you need to tell the judge in court, and everything else. You can ask Liam if he's willing to accompany you, but I'll give you all the knowledge you need, to feel comfortable with fighting this."

"Why? Because that keeps my contract cleaner for your family's law firm?"

A whisper of hurt flashed across his face. "Because this is a bullshit move on the best of days, but especially when it's directed at you. People like this need to be shut down. Besides, I'm biased and don't want to see you miserable."

At any hands other than your own. The bitter thought surged forward without her permission. "When do you have time?"

"Right now. My afternoon is free."

Please don't let me regret this. She gestured to the couch. "Can I get you a drink? There's Mt. Dew."

"I'd love that." He grinned. "Grab your laptop or something, to make notes with. We have a few hours of work ahead of us."

She returned with soda and computer in hand, and settled in next to him.

For the rest of the afternoon, he shoved her head full of so much knowledge, she thought her brain might explode. But she was grateful for the information. What felt daunting and overwhelming when Josh arrived now looked manageable. Another inconvenience at the office.

Someone knocked, and when Sydney looked up, she realized how low the sun had set in the sky. "Be right back." She crossed the room.

When she saw Dylan through the peephole, flutters danced through her heart. She flung the door open, threw her arms around his neck, and kissed him.

He wasn't kissing back. Why was he just standing there?

She stepped back, to ask what was wrong. He

wasn't looking at her; he was glaring at Josh, who appeared settled and completely at ease on her couch.

Well, fuck.

Dylan had a long day. The meeting with Sydney had left his mind whirring. He worked through lunch on a different project. And work kept him late.

Then to show up here, to find…

He wasn't jumping to conclusions. He also wasn't blind. Sydney was in a great mood when she greeted him. Josh looked entirely too at home in her living room. The two people who parted very bitter ways last night seemed to be getting along great now.

Dylan couldn't ignore the slap-in-the-face feeling that came with this. Worse, no one was saying anything. "Am I interrupting?" he asked.

"Not at all. Come in," Sydney said.

"Sure." He settled into a chair.

Josh's position on the couch and the paperwork spread out around him implied he and Sydney had been cozied up, doing… something.

Dylan fought the urge to be the possessive who flew off the handle. "What did I miss?" Either everything or nothing, given that there were no protests of *this isn't what it looks like*.

Sydney stood at the edge of the living room, looking between them. She crossed one arm across her chest, to grab the other. At least she had the grace to know this was an awkward situation. Josh didn't look fazed. "I was served a Cease and Desist for a patent infringement," she said.

The news worried Dylan on her behalf. He was also more than a little hurt she'd gone to Josh. "You could have called me. Or asked Liam about it."

"He hasn't contacted me yet."

"Oh." Dylan would deal with that later.

"And Josh was more or less here when I was served, so he got caught in the beam of my initial panic."

That didn't make the situation better in any way. "I'm sorry… Did I miss something? We ended last night with him telling you to pretend we don't know each other—not the least romantic thing to tell someone after sex, but probably in the top ten—and today he just happened to be here when you were served."

"I had the afternoon off, for the chiropractor." Josh finally spoke. "I stopped by, after—"

"Nope." Dylan snapped out the word. "I don't want to hear it from you." With Sydney, he didn't have the same gnawing concern she'd feed him bullshit. Which was a disconcerting feeling. He'd never mistrusted Josh before now.

"He wasn't here when I was served," Sydney said. "He showed up a few minutes after. I swear to God, it was one of those coincidences. He said he was here to apologize. I didn't want to hear it, but he saw me freaking out and offered to help. I might not trust him when it comes to keeping his commitments, but he grew up in that law firm, and if he says he's got an answer, I believe it."

Dylan didn't miss the hurt that flashed across Josh's face, and smugness surged inside. He could be the bigger guy here, but he wasn't up for that. He gestured for Sydney to come closer. "You should sit. It's been a long day." This setup still didn't sit well with him.

Sydney drew within arm's reach, and Dylan tugged her to sit in his lap. Her warm weight pressed against him. This might have been a bad idea, with the way his body was reacting. He didn't let his dick talk for him, though. Usually. "What was this about a C and D?"

"Patent troll is claiming Sydney stole their idea," Josh said, before Sydney could reply. "I was showing her why it wasn't a big deal.

So nothing was going on. That didn't stop Dylan's jealousy the way he wanted. "Why did you two break up?" It was a tangent, and it was a little manipulative. He wanted to remind them why they weren't together.

He'd heard snippets about their split. It wrecked Josh. He'd never pried for details before, though.

Sydney leaned into him. "Josh should tell you."

"You're the one who did the breaking, though. Am I right?"

"I was the one who said we were done. I wouldn't say I was responsible for all of the breaking. And after last night, I'm not sure he realizes even now why I walked away." Her sneer was audible.

Dylan wrapped an arm around her waist. Whatever happened this afternoon, he probably didn't need to worry about it. He still wanted answers.

"I *did* come over here to apologize." Josh sounded defensive.

"For…" Sydney dragged the word out.

Josh sighed. "She broke up with me because there was a really big moment—"

Sydney cleared her throat

"—and it wasn't the first one—that, due to a series of unfortunate events, I missed."

"You missed them *all*. After about three months of dating, you never made a single important date." Sydney's aggravation was growing.

Dylan wrapped an arm around her waist, for comfort, as much as to be possessive. He was building a bigger picture about her past with Josh, and he didn't have concerns about her intentions. Josh's, though…

Dylan would hate to choose between a friend and

a woman, and he'd regret if the choice was obvious and he'd never seen it coming.

"It wasn't *all*." Josh's protest was weak.

Sydney clenched her fist. "It was all. My birthday. *Your* birthday. Our graduation party. Dinner with my boss at the time. Our anniversary. Every single one of them because something came up that Laurie Hunter needed help with, and it was so critical, it had to be Josh helping, and it couldn't wait."

"What was the final straw?" Dylan was morbidly curious. "Not that I'd blame you if it was waking up one morning and realizing he was an asshole.

Sydney focused her pointed glare on Josh.

He ducked his head. "We were supposed to go to dinner, and then ring shopping after.

Ring shopping? An invisible fist clenched around Dylan's chest.

"We'd agreed not to call ourselves *engaged* until I was wearing the ring," Sydney said. "Instead of picking one out, I sat in the restaurant alone for a fucking hour, nibbling on bread and drinking my weight in water. There was no call. No hint as to where Josh was. And no answer when I tried to get a hold of him."

"I was taking notes in a last-minute critical deposition that ran over. I wasn't comfortable interrupting."

Dylan was still processing that Josh and Sydney had been essentially engaged. "You couldn't say, *give me two minutes to call my all-but fiancée and tell her why I'm late?*"

"Or better, you couldn't have told your lovely mother to get another fucking intern to take the notes?" Sydney leaned forward, anger dripping from her words.

"It was an critical client." Josh's protest was stronger than it should be.

Sydney stood, face twisted in anger. "They were *all* critical, weren't they? Every time Laurie needs you to do something, it's a *critical* thing that she only trusts you to handle. And it happened frequently enough that you missed every important date we had across more than a year. You bitch that she treats you worse than anyone else there, but apparently her fucking firm would collapse if you weren't around to meet with every important client who walks through her doors. I guess that explains why you were pulled from my contract negotiation."

Actually, it probably did, just not in the way she thought. Had Laurie Hunter worked to keep Josh and Sydney apart, for some reason?

"It's my career." Josh's voice rose.

Sydney growled. "I was supposed to be your fucking wife." She was shouting now. "And it's not your career. You don't even want to work there."

She had a good point, but Dylan wasn't going to interrupt. Sydney had this on her own. It was sexy-scary in the best way possible. It was easier to lean in that direction, than acknowledge that her rage may mean she still had feelings for Josh.

"I'm not going to half-ass a job just because it's not my final stop," Josh said.

Ouch. Wrong answer.

"No. You're just going to half-ass a relationship with the woman you said you wanted to spend your life with." Sydney's face was red.

If Dylan didn't step in now, would this come to blows? He was having trouble finding any sympathy for Josh at this moment.

14

Josh was digging himself into a deeper hole the longer he talked. Any minute now, his ego would stop blocking that message from his brain, and he'd apologize and back down.

He'd been in the wrong with Sydney. There were so many better ways he could have handled things back then, without sacrificing his job or his work ethic. Now was his chance to own it.

"I fucked up. I'm sorry." That wasn't as tough as he expected. It only burned a little.

Sydney raised an eyebrow. It was the least angry thing about her blotched red face, clenched jaw, and narrowed eyes.

"You could have at least tried not to wince when you'd said that." Dylan's tone was flat.

Josh swallowed a growl, as reason warred with pride in his thoughts. "What do you want me to say?"

"Until about thirty seconds ago, I would have

answered, *I just want an apology*. I'd like to amend that with, *it would be nice if you meant it."* Sydney gave him a thin-lipped smile.

Josh forced himself to take a deep breath and squash the obnoxious voice shouting, *she doesn't get it*. Because she did. Sydney was observant and intelligent and fun and creative. She'd never asked him to do something like quit his job or put it in jeopardy. She wanted his time for special occasions. He was the one who had been unreasonable.

"I'm sorry. Not for every single time. I won't say that, because it's not true. But you're right that I let work get in the way. Especially on those days like our anniversary, your birthday, our engagement. I'm sorry." That felt a lot better.

"Which ones aren't you sorry for?" Sydney countered.

Josh was prepared for that. "I never wanted to meet your boss. You didn't even go that night. I was the perfect excuse."

Sydney quirked her mouth in an unformed smile. "That's true. But it's not the point."

"How long do we do this for?" Dylan asked. His flat expression implied he wasn't going to forgive as quickly.

Wish I had your girlfriend back, and then feel like a dick for wanting to break you two up? Josh pushed the question aside. "Do what?"

"This back and forth, with the awkward running into each other. The arguing. The apologies. The hints of sexual tension." Dylan didn't sound amused.

Sydney leaned back into Dylan and gave him her full attention. "I'd suggest you and I spend more time here, but…"

"That's not the best solution." Dylan finished with a sigh.

Sydney shook her head. "Exactly. I can't ask you to never go home when you and I are spending time together."

Josh was doing exactly what he swore he wouldn't. He was coming between them. "I'm not…" What? The answer stuck in his throat. He wanted Sydney back. For the last few years he'd tried to ignore their past. Tell himself they were done.

After last night… he couldn't do that anymore. But he didn't want to come between her and Dylan. It was too bad they couldn't share.

Share had a nasty flavor to it. Sydney wasn't a piece of meat. It was too bad they couldn't all be together.

"You're not what?" Dylan hadn't loosened his grip on Sydney's waist, and his patience sounded thin.

"I'm not trying to come between you." That was about as true and real as this got.

Dylan looked skeptical. "If I were someone else, would you still say the same?"

Absolutely not. "If you were anyone else, Sydney would deserve better."

"Hi. Still here." Sydney waved her fingers. "I don't

remember asking either one of you who I was or wasn't allowed to date."

"Technically... I have a say in that." Dylan nuzzled her neck.

She rolled her eyes, but her smile had broken through. "All right, *technically.*"

Josh missed having that with her. An ache squeezed his heart. "This is going to sound weak, because it's so cliché, but... I'd like to be friends."

"Too bad..." Sydney frowned, then shook her head. "You're still an obsessive asshole about work. But tentative friends sounds good."

That hurt. He deserved it, but it stung. She also didn't finish the thought the way she wanted to. "What were you going to say?"

SYDNEY FELT DYLAN'S GRIP TIGHTEN ON HER HIP WHEN she said, *Too bad...* Did he know what she was thinking? Either way, she was glad he'd stopped her from saying too much.

What Kathryn had with her two guys was enviable in a lot of ways. Not just the not having to choose, but also the adoration. If Sydney trusted Josh, she might look for that with him and Dylan, but her mind was on the physical side of things. Diving into sex with Josh, just for that rush of being with two men again, was a bad idea.

And if she wanted to do any additional experimenting, she should be on the same page as Dylan. She needed to talk to him, anyway. Any sort of long-term relationship with him meant an agreement when it came to her ex and his roommate.

She stood and grasped Dylan's fingers. "Can I talk to you in the kitchen?"

"I can just cover my ears," Josh said.

Dylan climbed to his feet. "Privacy sounds like a good idea."

Sydney looked at Josh. This had gotten complicated fast. "Could you wait in the guest room?" It was the farthest room in the apartment from the kitchen, and the door closed. She'd ask him to leave, but they needed to work some of this out now. It was going to keep coming up either way.

"Sure." Josh frowned, but headed into the other room anyway.

The instant she heard the door latch shut, she pulled Dylan into the kitchen. The words wouldn't come, though. She paced, trying to organize her out-of-control thoughts.

Dylan stepped up behind her and rested his hands on her hips, interrupting her. He didn't pull her close, but the contact was comforting and helped her focus.

"Tell me what you're thinking," he said.

That was a bad idea. First of all, she'd have to put it into words, and then those words would need to form a coherent sentence. "You first."

"I don't think that's quite fair, but all right." He spun her to face him. "Josh is my best friend. He's been there for me, even though we've only known each other for a few years."

She nodded. That didn't change the way Josh had treated her.

Dylan guided her backward, until she collided with the counter. "Even though I've never seen the side of him that you did, I don't doubt you for a second, and you didn't deserve that. I'd like to think he's not that person, but apparently at least part of him still is," he said.

"Thanks for the support." She let out a strained laugh.

"Honestly, I kind of want to pound his face in, for treating you that way. I know how much it hurt him when you left, but that's on him, not you. I can also see he's still not over you."

Sydney didn't like the skip behind her ribs at hearing that. "I'm not giving him another chance. What he did was inconsiderate, but it wasn't abusive. Maybe he'll change, maybe not. I'm not looking at any of that. I'm concerned about you and me. I can't ask you not to talk to him anymore, and that means we'll all keep running into each other."

"You'd fuck him again."

She winced, but she wouldn't deny it. "It would be a mistake. There are too many blurred lines between then and now."

"So hook him up with one of your friends." Dylan pressed closer.

Jealousy jolted through her. "No. Not after what

he did to me. My point is, I only see two options." *Please don't let this be a mistake*. She was trying to be reasonable. To look at the situation from a rational perspective.

Dylan raised his brows.

"I either go out of my way to avoid him, or I learn to be friends with him." That made sense, didn't it?

Dylan dropped his hands from her hips. "I can't believe you're considering friendship, after what he did." The low seductive understanding vanished from his voice.

Was she really hearing this? It took her a moment to process the words. Was it her, or was that a hint hypocritical? "But you were okay with me fucking him? Are you considering ending your bromance with him?"

"No." The refusal carried a sharp edge.

"Because you've never personally witnessed him being that kind of an asshole, until last night?" Sydney crossed her arms. She was willing to give Josh another chance, if he was trying. Not more than one. But Dylan was making it sound like she was wrong to consider forgiveness, where it was fine for him. That was bullshit.

Dylan jammed his hands in his pockets. "You make a fair point. I suppose that means there's a third option."

"What's that?" Her gut twinged, telling her not to ask the question.

"You and I stop seeing each other." Dylan made it

sound like the simplest thing ever. "Then you don't have to worry about any of it."

Disbelief rang in her ears, and she swallowed back the bile rising in her throat. What just happened? How did they go from a reasonable conversation to this? "What?"

"It's been less than a week." How did he sound so fucking calm? Was this really the same guy who insisted over and over that he wanted to see where things went? "Don't misunderstand. You're sexy, fun, intelligent, and creative as fuck. But it's obvious you two aren't over each other. I can't compete with that kind of baggage."

Now this was her fault? "But—"

"Are you going to deny it?"

"I told you I'm not going back to him." Sydney couldn't keep the defensiveness from her retort.

"That's not what I said. Look me in the eye and tell me you're over him. Say that you don't wonder *if he changed, would I give him another chance*?"

Hadn't she said that? "Why are you turning this on me?"

"I'm not." His jaw was tight, and so were his words. He raked his fingers through his hair. "But this is how it looks from my perspective. You dumped this guy three years ago. He still wants you. And now you're asking me to watch and ignore all of that, so you two can *be friends*."

"Is this about how Josh feels now, or about how he treated me then? Or are you looking for excuses, because you don't want to admit I have a past before you?" That was probably a low blow. She was taking focus off the original issue as much as he was. "Because *this is how it looks from my perspective.*" She couldn't keep the snideness from her voice. "You want me to back off and rearrange how I do things, so I can date you but never run into Josh. But it's okay for you to stay his friend."

"Because I never—"

"Never loved him? Never stood by his side while he did something asinine? There's no one in this room who can say that. But this isn't about you, right? It's all about me. Because he was cruel to me. Because he still carries a flame for me. It seems like I'm not the one whose perspective is clouded by my past with Josh."

"He treated you wrong."

And they were back to that. "Yeah. He did. And it's up to me to say if I forgive me. You don't get to tell me that, especially if you're doing exactly the opposite of what you're advising me of." This was so bullshitty, she couldn't process it. "You know what? You're right. I like your third option. We're done."

A voice inside her head screamed, *What are you doing?* She wouldn't take it back, but she did want Dylan to. Why didn't he understand? Or was she the one being unreasonable?

He nodded. "So we agree. Finally. Have a nice life." He turned on his toe and strode from the kitchen. "You can come out now," he called. "I don't care what you do after that."

A heartbeat later, the front door opened and shut.

Sydney's heart cracked. She leaned back against the counter, waiting for the tears to fall. But there was nothing to alleviate her emptiness, disappointment, and hurt.

15

Sydney's mind was a jumbled wreck. What just happened? She slid to the floor, unable to process how quickly the situation deteriorated.

Josh paused in the doorway, studying her with concern. "What's going on?"

"You need to go." She couldn't deal with human interaction right now. Especially him, being considerate.

"What's wrong?" He stepped toward her.

"Now, please. I won't ask again."

He held up his hands, palms out as if surrendering, and shook his head. "You know where to find me if you need me."

She did, and that was part of the problem. She'd ignored him all this time, and suddenly he was in her life again, reminding her of both the good and bad.

The front door opened and closed for a second time.

She summoned all the numbness she could find and forced it through her veins. Her eyes stung, and her stomach hurt, but tears wouldn't come. She could only stare at the floor and ask, *What happened?*

DYLAN DIDN'T MEAN FOR THAT TO FALL APART. He replayed the argument over and over, as he stalked to his car and headed home.

This was the right decision. Regardless of how hard his heart and body pushed back, he was doing what he needed to. There was too much baggage between Josh and Sydney. Too much of a past to get sucked into and bogged down by.

And you're jealous.

He rolled his eyes at the counter argument. Jealous of what? Of Josh?

And maybe Sydney, a little. That thing they have…

So?

He enjoyed Sydney's company and the sex. Maybe they'd fall in love, given enough time, and maybe not. But he wasn't doing this back-and-forth thing with her and Josh. He couldn't watch her go back to a guy who treated her badly.

You mean your best friend? The guy you're pretty sure knows better, so you're staying with him?

Dylan cranked the stereo, to drown out his thoughts.

If Sydney kicked Josh out after Dylan left, he wouldn't be far behind.

Would facing him at home be worse than Josh not coming home right away? Was he still at Sydney's?

If she thought it wasn't possible to ignore Josh while he was living with Dylan, Dylan would prove her wrong. At least for a few days. He needed to get his head on straight.

When he got home, he headed straight to his room and locked the door.

Less than five minutes later, Josh knocked. "Do you have a minute? Do you want to talk?"

At least he didn't stick around at Sydney's. Dylan saw no flaws with that.

"No and no," Dylan called. The best thing for him to do was get back to life as it was before.

He tried to read. Watch movies. Do a little studying for work. His head was too busy arguing with itself, for him to focus on anything.

He left early in the morning, but not before writing Josh a quick note. *I need to process. Give me time.*

Dylan's brain countered with, *You couldn't do the same for Sydney? She's not the one who was an asshole.*

Sydney made her decision.

After you forced her hand.

He had a long day of work ahead of him. This was

a bad time to fall onto an upgraded merry-go-round of mental arguing.

Dylan managed to avoid Josh most of the day, at home and at work. By lunchtime on Thursday, he was willing to admit Sydney had at least one thing right—it was almost impossible to not run into Josh while Dylan was living with him.

And now Sydney was back in his thoughts. The empty pit in his chest that he'd tried to ignore for days throbbed with longing.

It had only been a week since he met her. Why did her not being here gnaw at him so much?

Wrong question.

The right one was, *Why did I walk away?*

Because you're jealous.

He needed to get his work done. Before he could second-guess himself, he had his phone out. He sent Sydney a quick text. *I need to talk to you.*

When she didn't answer immediately, he dove back into the tasks he got paid for.

Dylan sifted through a stack of paperwork for one of Aaron's cases, making notes as appropriate. He flipped past one page, and a line of text caught his attention out of the corner of his eye.

What did he just read?

He scanned the paragraph several times, but nothing about it looked out of place. Nagging tickled his thoughts, telling him to look closer. That wasn't helpful without more information.

He moved on.

By Friday after work, he needed to crawl out of his head before he went insane. Between ignoring Josh and not hearing back from Sydney, his brain was a hazardous wasteland.

What was he going to do with his weekend? Most of the time, he'd game with Josh. Sometimes he'd hook up, but it had been a while. There was no reason to spend his time studying for the bar or for school.

Maybe he'd go out and get drunk. Get past this funk. If he and Sydney were over, there was nothing wrong with that. Hell, they'd never officially started.

Josh was gone when Dylan got home.

Dylan didn't care where. He changed into a more casual shirt and headed out.

He was so busy, avoiding his own thoughts as he drove, he didn't realize he was near Sydney's apartment complex until the sign came into view.

What was he doing?

Turning into the parking lot apparently, rather than heading to the club.

Not that it mattered. Her car wasn't here.

He continued on his original path. What would have happened if they hadn't split? He'd have to deal with these questions eventually. If he sorted through them, could he move on?

What if Dylan and Sydney had talked past the rough spot? What if he'd watched her try to be friends with Josh? What if he'd watched her deny they were more than friends?

He clenched the steering wheel until his knuckles ached.

They could do away with that denial. Admit up front that more was possible.

That would hurt. Dylan couldn't pretend otherwise. He didn't want to be on the outside of Sydney and Josh's relationship.

Would you rather be in the middle?

His own question caught him off guard. Was that an option? Because he should mind the idea, but it felt better than anything else he'd asked about this situation all week.

Could he share? Sydney or Josh?

The alternative was cutting at least one of them out of his life.

Fuck.

When he reached the bar, it was loud inside. Distracting. Impossible to think. Perfect.

He ordered a Sprite.

You're here to drink and get laid. You're already failing on Point One.

He didn't want to leave his car here. It meant either taking a cab or calling Josh for a ride.

One song bled into the next while he nursed his drink. The girl at the other end of the bar was cute and watching him over her glass. It would take minimal effort to wave the bartender over and order her another of whatever she was drinking.

She wasn't Sydney.

He pulled a ten from his wallet for drink and tip, and walked away. Most expensive Sprite ever.

The entire drive home, his brain rehashed the same old questions. Could he watch Sydney be friendly—more—with Josh? Was he willing to see how things went if the two of them resumed their relationship?

Not if it left Dylan out. But that wasn't what Sydney had asked. Never once. It might be what she meant, but she'd been honest with him so far. She'd only asked why he held his relationship with Josh to a different standard than hers.

Back home, there was a note from Josh on the fridge that he wouldn't be back tonight.

Thank God. Not that Dylan wanted him gone forever. But he needed to sort out his head.

The knock startled him. Who was visiting at nine at night?

He opened the door to find Sydney on the other side.

Her expression was unreadable, but she looked good. Sexy. Curvy. Fuckable.

He shoved it all down. "Hey."

"I wouldn't have come up if Josh's car was here. You wanted to talk?"

The text he sent yesterday. He did want to talk. There was so much to say. Impulse swept through him. He knotted his fingers in her hair and crushed his mouth to hers.

Sydney whimpered against his lips. She planted

her hands on his chest and pushed him back. "I said *talk.*"

"Right." Dylan still tasted her. Her scent drilled into his thoughts. Was he supposed to go first?

You could apologize.

Sydney crossed her arms. He didn't register his gaze falling to her chest until she cleared her throat and shoved her hands in her pockets instead. "You're right. I'm not over Josh. Maybe I'm dumb for hoping he's changed, but I won't apologize for how I feel," she said.

Nothing Dylan didn't already know. He met her gaze. "Okay."

She twisted her mouth. Did she expect something else?

"Now it's your turn," she said.

"I'm sorry." For the first time in days, his brain wasn't assaulting him with questions. "I know why you're mad, and you're right. I can't expect you to hate him for something I excuse. I want to make things work between you and me. I don't know how to get past this and back to where we were."

"We start by admitting this is a really convoluted situation. The kind of thing that gets called *implausible* in books and movies. The type of fucked up that only happens in real life."

Dylan nodded. He agreed.

"And then you promise me that if we finish that kiss, it doesn't lead to us fucking and then you kicking me out."

He twitched his fingers, wanting to grab her again. Feel her. Lose himself in her. "I'm not kicking you out."

"If I asked you to kick Josh out, would you?" Her expression was still unreadable, but her voice hitched.

Dylan was caught off guard by the question. He already knew the answer, though. "No. But I also won't ask you to do anything similar. I truly am sorry."

She twisted her mouth, then caught her bottom lip between her teeth. The shift made her that much more alluring. "All right. You can kiss me."

He didn't need to hear more. He gripped the back of her neck and nipped her lips before kissing her hard.

She groaned. Fuck, he missed that sound. She grabbed fistfuls of his shirt and pressed her body closer.

Dylan was so not ready to surrender whatever this was. He didn't care what they called it, as long as he was a part of it.

He tugged her into the apartment, never breaking the kiss, and kicked the door shut behind him.

She pressed her fingers to his lips, interrupting the moment. "So are we good?"

"We're wonderful." He drew one finger into his mouth and sucked.

Her groan drilled into his thoughts. Her softness teased every inch of his body.

"We can keep talking if you want," he said. He

tried to push her away, to play, but his body refused to cooperate. "But I think we'll both be happier once I get you naked and I'm worshiping those gorgeous curves of yours."

Sydney tugged his shirt over his head. "You've sold me."

He shoved up her top, pushing her bra out of the way in the process, and lowered his head. He dragged his tongue over a nipple, before drawing it into his mouth to suck and nibble.

She groaned and ground into him.

"I missed you," he murmured against her breast. "How did you get under my skin so fast?"

Sydney's giggle was another high, mingling with the pleasant cloud in his head. She snaked her hand down his chest and traced his erection through his jeans. "Pretty sure I made my luck roll."

"You're so perfectly geeky." He claimed her mouth again. He couldn't get enough. "And delicious. Did I mention that?"

"It's the bubblegum glamour. It makes me yummy."

He nipped down her neck, to bite her shoulder. "Very tasty." He pulled her shirt and bra off the rest of the way and tossed them aside.

"Are we going to be okay?" A hint of hesitation slid into her light tone.

He hoped so. He couldn't promise, though. "I think we can get back to where we were, and keep moving forward."

"Diplomatic of you." Her teasing was back. "I should stop asking tough questions until you're not looking to get laid."

He kneaded her breast, enjoying the splash of emotions on her face. "You can ask me anything you want. Now or later." The conversation didn't diminish his desire. He wanted to explore her and talking at the same time.

Sydney dragged down his zipper and stroked him through his boxer briefs. The thin layer of fabric between her skin and his was maddening in the best way possible.

"I still don't know what to do about..." She ducked her head. "About Josh. About you. I just knew I needed to see you."

Dylan should be jealous that Josh's name was still coming up, while they were half-naked. He didn't mind, though. "No one ever said the other night can't happen again." What the fuck was he saying?

She pulled back, her furrowed brow reflecting his mental question. "What did you say?"

16

Sydney thought she was keeping up with the conversation and Dylan's attentions, until he threw that curve ball out there. It was good. Incredible even. But she didn't know what to do with his statement.

"I don't know if I can stand to see you with other guys, but..." He muffled his words by kissing along her shoulder.

Heat and electricity raced over her skin, and desire thrummed underneath. She wasn't sure she should ask. Turned-on plus trepidation made for an odd cocktail. "But what?"

"But Josh is different."

Her breath caught in her throat. Was she upset that Dylan brought the conversation back to Josh while he was feeling her up, or grateful that she didn't have to be the one to do it? She didn't dare make any assumptions. "I don't know what you're implying. You have to spell it out for me."

"I don't know what I'm saying either, except… the other night was a lot of fun." He trailed a finger under the band of her jeans, tempting her.

She sucked in a sharp breath when he traced along her hip. "If you were upset that I'm not over him, Round Two won't make things better."

"I understand. I've had a few days to think about it." Dylan unbuttoned and unzipped her pants. "I'm okay with it." He pushed her jeans to the floor, then teased along the crotch of her panties.

This was distracting and delicious. Was she thinking clearly? The hammering of her heart against her ribs made it hard to say. He didn't hesitate with his assurance. There was no, *I think…*

She pressed into his touch. She was wet and anxious. Did she want him to finger her or fuck her? All of the above.

The front door *snicked*, and her heart leaped into her throat.

Josh walked in and paused, gaze locked on hers. He twisted his mouth. "Well, *fuck*."

Sydney should cover up, but she didn't want to stop. Desire pulsed in her veins. This wasn't the litmus test she would have picked, but it was an interesting way to see if Dylan meant what he said.

"So you're okay with things happening again?" She forced the question out, keeping it quiet enough for his ears only. She was about to completely destroy things if she pushed wrong. She was intensely aware of Josh watching them.

Dylan rested his forehead against hers. He murmured, "What if I say *no?* At least not yet?"

That was fair. More than reasonable. "He betrayed me, and there's a lot to atone for there. You didn't. If you say *no,* that's all I need to hear."

"And if I say, *let's see where this goes?*" He brushed his lips over hers, his volume normal again.

"Where what goes?" Josh asked.

What were the odds she could have something like what Kathryn had? Two guys, all the time? She shouldn't hope for that, or that Josh would redeem himself, but she couldn't help it. Why was she so willing to make dumb mistakes when it came to Josh?

Because she knew the good, as well as the bad. And if Dylan was okay with things…

"Do you want an audience?" Dylan's question interrupted her off-the-rail thoughts but didn't erase them. His attention was fully on her.

She caught her bottom lip between her teeth. "*God,* yes."

"Since neither of you is speaking directly to me, I need to pick between staying and going." Josh's voice was thick, as he flicked his gaze between Sydney and Dylan.

Dylan raised his brows. "You're still here. Haven't you already made that choice?"

Josh shook his head. "No. But I don't have a

problem admitting I'm enjoying the view while someone makes up their mind."

Memories joined the fantasy and heat racing through Sydney's veins—the way she felt in the hentai viewing room, with Dylan's hands roaming her body, while others watched. This was a show for one, but it made her heart hammer against her ribs harder than when they'd been interrupted in the hotel.

"You should stay," she said to Josh. "But you have to promise to keep your hands to yourself." Like that was going to make the situation less of a bad idea.

The thrum of need between her legs didn't care, and, neither did she.

Josh held up his hands. "I promise the only person I'll touch is myself."

He took a seat in the chair across from them. His half-smirk sent ripples of desire along her tender nerves.

Dylan pressed his chest to her back and glided his hands up her stomach, to cup her breasts. He kneaded gently as he kissed along her neck.

She groaned and pressed back into him. His hard length dug into her back, teasing and tempting. Between that and the way Josh stroked himself through his jeans, Sydney was squirming again.

Dylan pinched one nipple, and she gasped at the sharp sting. He rolled the swollen nub between his fingers, alternating between heavy and light pressure, while he slid his other hand down her stomach, to dip below her panties.

He slipped his fingers between her folds. "*Fuck,* I love how much this turns you on." His growl vibrated against her skin.

"Me too." Her laugh ended in a moan. She bucked her hips when he brushed her clit.

He moved away, teasing along her slippery skin, but not offering relief.

When Josh unzipped and worked himself free, a new shock of desire spilled inside and throbbed between her legs.

Dylan finally moved up to the center of her need, tracing circles around her clit. He teased and coaxed, edging away each time her groans grew more punctuated.

She hovered in the knife edge of pleasure, whimpering and grinding, needing release.

Disappointment mingled with desire and release when Dylan pulled both hands away. She didn't have time to process what he was doing, before he hooked his thumbs in her panties and dragged them down to her knees.

She wriggled to drop them further

"They're good where they are." Dylan slapped her ass.

The sharp sting amplified her arousal.

He wedged a foot between hers and twisted, widening her stance. It wasn't the same as being bound, but the stretchy cotton was a tantalizing restraint.

Josh watched it all, stroking slowly, lips slightly parted.

Dylan pressed a hand into the small of her back, prompting her to bend over the couch. He trailed his hand along her behind. "*God,* I love watching your ass. And all of you, but this view is pretty incredible." He slipped two fingers between her legs and dipped into her opening.

She clenched at the easy intrusion. No witty responses came to mind. Once again, he had her tongue-tied and her thoughts racing with anticipation.

He withdrew, and she heard the tear of foil.

Dylan nudged her opening with the head of his cock, then slipped inside easily. He stretched her out and filled her up.

She pressed back into his cock, wanting him buried deep.

"*Fuck,* you feel good." He gripped her hips hard and withdrew almost all the way, before driving inside her again. The slow tease built rapidly to a hard pounding, as he slammed into her.

The combination of everything—the lingering touches on her skin, Josh stroking himself quickly, Dylan hammering against her—built back to the cusp of climax.

Dylan pried his fingers from her skin, to reach around. He sought out her clit again. When he brushed the tender nub, she squeezed around his shaft. He rubbed on either side.

The caress was enough to coax orgasm from her. She came hard, clenching his erection and the back of the couch.

He didn't ease up, and she fell into the stars that danced behind her eyelids. She watched as Josh came. That she'd been his private show was enough to draw out her pleasure.

Dylan's grunts grew shorter and more punctuated, matching his hard pace. He let out one final groan and slowed to a stop.

She didn't want to climb down from this cloud. Up here it was amazing and warm, and her thoughts were fuzzed, and out there, she might have to choose.

For now, she was only focusing on this moment. What lay beyond was too uncertain.

17

Josh should have turned and walked out the instant he saw Sydney and Dylan mostly naked in the living room. A feat easier said than done, when the view was so fantastic.

When they invited him to stay, there was no way he could say *no*.

"Do I dare ask what I missed?" He wasn't content to sit in his lonely seat anymore. He wanted to be part of the tangle of limbs on the couch.

He crossed the room, and Sydney scooted her legs without hesitation to make room for him. He sat and pulled her feet in to his lap.

Dylan glanced at her, brows raised in question.

Sydney shrugged. "Part of what we discussed was about him."

Now Josh was really curious.

Dylan wrapped an arm more tightly around Sydney. "We were arguing about why it was okay for me to be friends with you but not her. Did I get that right?"

"You did." The tiny smile on her face was the pleased, content expression Josh used to adore.

Fuck, he still did. But he didn't like the knot that grew in his throat at Dylan's words. He didn't want to lose that friendship.

Or more.

What was that supposed to mean? "And the conclusion was I can watch you have sex?"

Sydney wrinkled her nose. "It sounds a lot more creepy and a lot less hot when you put it that way. I want… wanted…"

Josh could guess what she was going to say, but he didn't dare.

"To restart from the last save point," Dylan said.

"That's catchy, but barely clearer. Are you going to start hanging a tie on the front door? Spending more and more time at her place?" That was the opposite of, *let's see where this goes,* but Josh needed them to say it. To vocalize that it was okay for him to be a part of their relationship, and to what extent.

The casual sex was fun, even only watching. But he didn't want to be a third wheel, and he had zero interest in being a sentient vibrator.

Dylan furrowed his brow. "Not unless that's what you prefer."

"I don't have more specific words for it." Sydney shifted her legs so more weight rested against Josh's. "*Let's see where this goes* doesn't rule anything out."

"But you're still dating him." Josh nodded at Dylan.

Sydney twisted her lips and was silent for a moment. "And you're still living together."

"It's not the same." Josh almost fumbled on the words. It wasn't. They were roommates.

"You sure? Because friends with occasional benefits sounds similar." Sydney held his gaze.

Okay, maybe he didn't want them to define it. No reason to take anything off the table. Sydney had a friend who dated two guys. It worked fine for them, regardless of how Josh felt about Kathryn on a personal level. "All right. I'm in for this ambiguous… whatever it is. Besides, I kind of like the idea of no rules."

Sydney and Dylan both laughed.

Josh didn't get the joke. "What?"

"You hate not having rules." A playful smirk danced on Sydney's lips.

God, she was so fucking kissable. Was that allowed?

Nothing was off the table.

He leaned in and brushed his mouth over hers. Familiar sparks. A desire he thought he remembered but had completely understated.

Sydney's gasp hummed through him, and she leaned into him, pressing more weight and hunger into the kiss.

Dylan's growl snapped them apart.

Josh had to fight, to keep from tracing the faint sting that lingered on his lips.

"Is that a *no*?" Sydney leaned back into Dylan, her question tentative.

Dylan brushed her hair from her neck and licked a path up to her earlobe. Her eyelids fluttered, and she sighed.

"It's not a *no*." Dylan's voice was muffled by her skin. "It's more of a, *Fuck, I liked watching that*."

Josh's blood heated to scalding with need. This was going to be interesting in the best way. "*Fuck*, I missed you, Tink."

Dylan traced a path down Sydney's arm, to tangle his fingers with hers. "You're staying here tonight."

"Okay." She nodded. "I didn't come prepared for that, so I don't have any extra clothes."

Josh was going to push this a little more. Not too much, but enough to get a loose idea of boundaries. "Oh darn." He kept the teasing in his sarcasm. "You might have to stroll around mostly naked for the next couple of hours."

"Crude." Dylan didn't sound upset. He handed Sydney his T-shirt. "We don't want you getting cold."

She tugged the top over her head. It was hard to tell when she was seated, but it looked like it was barely going to cover her ass.

There was a sting of jealousy that she was in Dylan's clothes, but the sight itself made up for it. "I was wrong." Josh was willing to admit it in this rare case. "That's *much* better than nude. Leaves just enough to the imagination and is easy to take off."

"Not that I mind the attention. *Wow,* I really don't. I almost don't know what to do with it." Sydney's chuckle was playful. "But I'm not a fuck-all-night kind of girl, so if you two are going to get it on tonight, I'm the one who gets to watch next round."

Josh gripped her fingers and kissed the tips. "I think we can behave for at least a couple of hours."

"I guess if you two are out, so am I." Dylan gave an exaggerated sigh, but he was smiling.

"In that case, I'm going to ruin the moment even further," Sydney said. "What am I going to do about this patent troll thing?"

"We'll write up a reply and hand it off to our friend." Dylan paused with a frown. "A different friend. One who will call you back."

Josh liked the plan, but it had a teensy, tiny, glaring flaw. "That's a huge legal gray area."

"We won't be acting against our client or the firm," Dylan said.

"Hence *gray area.*" Was this another of those instances that had upset Sydney before? Putting work before them? No. This was actually toeing a line, not putting in a few extra hours at work. But Josh wanted to help, and they wouldn't handle the actual interaction, just point her in the right direction. "I'm not saying we shouldn't. We just need to draw that line, for everyone's safety."

"I'm grateful for all of it. Don't get yourselves in

trouble, but thank you for everything," Sydney said.

Dylan grinned. "Good. We'll get you sorted in the morning."

They tripped from one subject to another, talking long into the night. When all three of them were yawning as much as anything else, Josh did something he was reluctant to do. "We should get to bed."

Which meant letting them vanish into Dylan's room, because they were the couple, and Josh would go sleep alone.

"I'm good here for a little longer." Sydney's protest was cut short by another yawn. She blinked several times. "I promise."

Dylan nodded. "Me too. Sleep is for the week, right?"

Josh remembered that mantra all too well, from the last several years of school. "Exactly." This was delaying the inevitable. For now, no matter how much he wanted otherwise, he was that third wheel.

He had another chance, though. An opportunity to earn Sydney's friendship again, even if it wasn't more, and he was going to reach for that for all he was worth.

Josh's neck screamed in protest at the angle he'd slept on it, forcing him awake. He pried his eyelids open, his body sending mixed signals of pleasure and pain.

A warm weight pressed against him. Partly Sydney's and partly Dylan's.

They'd fallen asleep on the couch, in an awkward jumble. *Fuck,* he'd missed waking up with her bare skin next to his. The entire night lingered fresh in his thoughts. He'd known he wasn't over Sydney, but spending this kind of time with her was a reminder of just how much he missed her company.

And things were getting back to normal with Dylan. That was nice. A few days of not speaking was too much for Josh.

He couldn't get up without disturbing them, but he needed to be in a different position. He extracted himself as carefully as possible, not surprised when both of them moaned and stirred.

Josh left them to find their own consciousness. He took a quick shower with the water on as cold as he could stand. He needed to keep his head clear, until he knew how this morning would play out after last night.

He ventured back into the living room, to catch the tail end of Dylan talking.

"…home, pack an overnight back, and we'll pick you up in an hour for breakfast."

They were making plans for their weekend. *We'll…* that implied Josh was a part of those plans. He liked that. "What if I don't want to go for breakfast?" He couldn't help teasing.

Sydney glanced at him over her shoulder, mouth

twisted. "Who are you, and what have you done with Josh?"

He struggled to keep his expression straight. "Maybe I've changed. A guy can't stay a diner-omelet junkie his entire life."

"Maybe not, but you haven't given it up yet," Dylan said.

Josh's smirk broke through. "Yeah, all right. I'm in."

They sent Sydney on her way, and Dylan vanished into his room.

Thank God Josh didn't have anything pressing today. He was focused intently on what happened last night. The sex. The words exchanged. What it all meant…

And the question that had nagged him for the last week, that he hadn't been able to resolve with Dylan avoiding him—what was going on with him and Dylan? Things were awfully rocky, for not letting this come between them.

Dwelling on things without talking them through wouldn't get Josh anywhere. Despite his arguments against helping Sydney with this patent-troll bullshit, he'd already looked things over with her. It would take ten minutes to type up a basic letter to the opposing party, and then he could hand it off to her.

Josh was wrapping up, when he heard doors opening from the direction of Dylan's bedroom. He padded to the room and leaned against the doorframe.

Dylan was pulling on a shirt. It was always an incredible sight.

"Are we good?" Josh asked.

Dylan grabbed a pair of socks from his drawer. "I don't know. We're not the same as we were a week ago."

Josh tempered his irritation. On the one hand, he hadn't done anything to Dylan. His actions three years ago shouldn't impact their lives now.

Then again, Josh had pulled that bullshit with Sydney the first night they were back together, and if he were in Dylan's shoes, he'd be furious to see someone else trying to force Sydney out of his life.

"Thank you for sticking with me," Josh said. "I won't make you or Sydney regret it."

Dylan finally paused to look at him. "That's what I'm banking on. No third chances."

Josh didn't care for the ultimatum, but there wasn't a lot of room for argument. "All right."

"Cool. So, last night. Hot, right?"

Except for the part where Josh was an outside observer. He didn't have an issue with watching; it was that there was no other option that he was wavering on. "Superhot."

"Gotta go get Sydney. Meet you there." Dylan clapped Josh on the shoulder as he brushed by.

How long was Josh willing to play third wheel, to figure this out?

Longer than a weekend. But only for Sydney… and Dylan.

Dylan liked intertwining his fingers with Sydney's as he drove them to the diner. A light and constant thrum flowed between them.

He shouldn't be okay with the arrangement last night. Logic and a lifetime of living in reality said, if he kept seeing Sydney and let Josh be a part of their relationship, it would end badly.

There should be reservations. He should hesitate.

It all felt all right, though. Would that change if they continued? If he found himself in the same place Josh was last night—watching?

Desire lit along his skin at the thought of sitting back and observing while Josh and Sydney fucked.

He shoved the image aside. If he lingered on the thought too long, he'd be fighting an uncomfortable erection.

He and Sydney reached their destination. As he

joined her on the sidewalk, his hand found hers again with little thought.

"I haven't been here in ages." Sydney's voice was soft.

Dylan wasn't surprised. He and Josh came here all the time. It was Josh's favorite place. "They have new menus."

"Did they add anything good?"

"They didn't add anything. They just printed new menus."

She laughed, and her posture relaxed. "At least I know what I'm getting, then."

Inside, Josh waved from the booth in the back of the dining room.

"New upholstery, too." Sydney bounced once as she slid into the seat. "I barely recognize the place."

As Dylan took the spot next to her, Josh passed his phone across the table. "I drafted you a response letter, for the Cease and Desist," Josh said.

"My hero." Sydney pretended to swoon. "Email it to me? Or this friend of yours? And thank you."

That almost made Dylan jealous. What happened to all the protests? But even with that thought, he was happier that Sydney was getting what she needed and Josh was involved.

Was that weird or normal?

Dylan didn't know anymore. He wanted this to be what it was. Could he have that?

"I've been wondering something." Sydney angled herself in her seat, one leg on the bench, so she was turned between them. Her leg pressed against Dylan's. "How do you go from roommates to, *Be my* plus one *at this important dinner*?"

Josh shrugged. "We just did."

"No. There has to be more to it than that."

"You did know he was into girls *and* guys?" Dylan rested a hand on her calf.

Her smile came easily. "That was part of what made the threesome idea more fun. But there has to be a story to it. You know I love a good story."

"There's really not." Josh leaned back as Mel, the waitress, brought them coffee and water. "I told her we all wanted our usual."

Mel looked at Sydney. "Lovely to see you again, dear. We missed you."

"I missed you too. And the usual is great."

Mel made sure they were set, and walked away.

"I'll give." Dylan prepared his coffee and took a tentative sip. Perfect. "There's technically a story, but it's not the kind of thing that brings audiences to their knees in laughter or tears. He needed a date for some event Laurie set him up for, and didn't want to go."

Josh leaned in. "Dylan said, *I'll go. That ought to ruffle some feathers*. And I liked the sound of it."

"Which led to, *You know what else would raise eyebrows? If we slept together*." Sydney watched them over the top of her mug as she sipped her coffee.

Dylan liked the amusement in her voice. "Not quite. That was more like, I was horny, he was horny, and it happened more than once." The explanation sounded too casual. Like a brush off. But it was the truth.

So why did Dylan wish there was more to it?

"You need to work on your storytelling skills," Sydney said. "Try this on for size. The strong, handsome warrior had suffered a long, hard day of work. His bones were weary—"

"And his bone needed attention." Josh smirked.

Sydney rolled her eyes and shook her head, but her smile never wavered. "Not what I was going for. You didn't want to tell the story before. Have you changed your mind?"

"He hasn't," Dylan said. "I'd rather hear your version."

"Because your bone needs attention?" Sydney leaned back in her seat.

Dylan followed her gaze to Mel, who had just arrived with their food. Kitchen-sink omelet for Josh, chocolate-chip pancakes for Dylan, and apparently a grilled-cheese sandwich for Sydney.

"My bone got attention." Dylan was sparse with the syrup, but glad there was a lot of butter for his pancakes. "I'm cocky enough to believe I can have the same again, whether or not Josh spins his Beavis and Butthead version of our sex life."

Sydney held up a finger, worked her jaw, then dropped her hand again. "So, one—pretty sure neither of them ever got laid. And two—which one does that make you?"

Dylan pulled his shirt up over the back of his head

and stuck his arms in the air, bent at the elbows and out to his sides. "Are you threatening me?"

"Oh my God." Sydney laughed. "I don't know if I needed to know how good you are at that."

"You needed to know. Because even when he's being asinine, he still does it perfectly." Josh's retort almost sounded affectionate. It wasn't enough to hide his irritation, though.

Dylan would bet it was because people were staring. He didn't care. He straightened his clothes. Inspiration struck. Did he have a lightbulb over his head, like in a cartoon? "You know what we need to do? Put our conversation from the other day to the test. See whether or not the three of us make a good questing party."

Josh seemed to consider this. "Someone has to DM. I nominate Tink."

"I accept. But two people don't make for much of a party…" Sydney drummed her fingers on the table. "Ooh, I can call Kathryn."

Josh scowled.

That was curious. "Who's Kathryn and what did I miss?"

"She's my best friend. You'll love her," Sydney said.

Josh's scowl deepened. "And she doesn't care for me."

Sydney pursed her lips and narrowed her gaze. "Do you blame her? You were an ass to me."

Josh clenched his jaw.

"This is your chance to prove her wrong." A sweet hint wove into Sydney's reply. She looked at Dylan again. "I promise. And you'll love her boyfriends, too."

Wait. *Boyfriends?* Did Dylan hear that right? "Call her. You're right. Two isn't really enough for a big campaign."

"I have the perfect one." Sydney grabbed her phone, poked the screen, then stuck it to her ear. "I've been sitting on it for way too long. Hey, it's me." Her tone and attention shifted. "What are you all doing today? … You up for a game? … More than just us. You know how I told you about that guy I met?"

She'd been talking about Dylan?

"That's the one." She frowned. "Both of them… It's just a game… I'm dating his roommate. It's going to happen."

The laughter faded from Josh's eyes, and his expression went flat.

There was a lot implied in Sydney's half of the conversation. Josh being relegated to *roommate* was probably the most glaring.

This was getting complicated. The one thing Dylan wanted to avoid. But he wasn't interested in walking away. Not yet.

Sydney set up a time with Kathryn, and gave her Dylan and Josh's address.

After breakfast, they headed back to the apartment to meet up, with a quick stop to buy snacks and soda.

When everyone showed up, introductions were

passed around. Kathryn and Josh glared at each other, and the guys with her didn't seem to care for him either. Kathryn was slender, with dark hair and light eyes, and there was a fluidity to her movement that Dylan recognized. It was similar to Josh's.

When Sydney said Kathryn was an Aikido black-belt and taught at a local dojo, that explained that.

Evan was the all-American blond boy, solid wall of muscle. He looked like the kind of guy who'd be cast as *Perfect Rebound Boyfriend Number One* on any TV show. He also looked like he was deciding if he could take Josh.

Trevor stayed close to Kathryn, arms crossed. He had dark hair, a wiry build, and looked like he'd bite anyone who came near her.

Especially Josh.

Sydney wasn't kidding about tension.

"Should we roll out characters?" Dylan would love a little bit of small talk. Fun. Build-up. If he was reading the room right at all, they needed to skip those at least until the glaring died down.

Sydney's tiny frown caught him off guard. "Do you need to?" she asked. "We can, definitely. Everyone else has a favorite already, but we can give you some extra stats, to put you…"

At their level. "I have one. I just figured, with a new campaign and since we've never played together before, you'd want that."

She shook her head. "I'm good to use existing. I'll adapt the story as we go. I just need your stats."

Dylan was impressed. And a bit annoyed with everyone else that they seemed to expect that answer. He'd never played with a DM before who didn't put hours into planning a campaign. And then reminded the players every time they screwed with a carefully crafted tale.

They settled around the living room like there was a divider wall running down the middle. Kathryn, Evan, and Trevor were distinctly keeping to their side.

Dylan had a barbarian character he loved to play. Dumb as a sack of rocks, but built like a tank. He amused himself with that pun.

When Josh said he was playing a healer, Kathryn laughed, and another round of glares was exchanged.

Kathryn played a monk, Evan a ranger, and Trevor a battle mage.

None of this seemed to surprise Sydney.

"We ready?" Sydney asked.

There was a series of nods and grunts. Dylan wanted to knock some heads together at the lack of enthusiasm, but he was willing to watch and wait.

Sydney wove a stunning setting of the countryside their party traveled through. With each question she asked, she received a round of one-word replies.

Josh continued to exchange glares with Kathryn. Sydney's tone wilted with each passing minute. Half an hour in, Dylan could almost hear her asking herself, *Why did I think this was a good idea?*

He was sick of this. Not of her. He suspected

Sydney's story had a lot of potential, if everyone would just play.

"You reach the edge of a forest." Sydney spoke in a near-monotone. "It stretches endlessly in front of you, as far as you can tell. The trees are green and dense and shit. You can continue on the road that goes around the forest, but you don't know how far the tree line extends." She gave a little sigh. "You can go through the forest, but the foliage is so overgrown, you can't see more than a few feet ahead."

"Can we camp for the night and wait to see if things are better in full sunlight?" Kathryn asked. It was the longest sentence she'd spoken since she arrived.

Josh shook his head. "I'm not camping with my back to that forest."

"What do you want to do instead?" Trevor narrowed his gaze. "If we go into the forest, more our backs are exposed."

"Then we'll backtrack enough to establish a perimeter." There was a bite in Josh's reply.

Evan made a disgusted grunt. "Do you even know what that means? We pushed hard to get this far this fast."

"No. We pushed hard because no one wants to make any decisions." Now Josh was just being snide. "I'm making a decision. I want to backtrack and set up where we have a good view of all of our surroundings."

Sydney's scowl deepened with each new retort.

This was so not better than the one-word answers.

Dylan was done. "I check for traps."

The swivel of heads in his direction was almost comical. He bit back the laugh.

"You don't have that skill in your character class," Trevor said.

"I can still look around, right? I'm capable of scanning the forest?" Dylan looked at Sydney.

"I..." She looked between the character sheets and him. "Your perception is three."

Dylan didn't care. "I want to check for traps."

"Where?" Sydney picked up the dice and rolled her thumb along them in her palm.

"In the forest." At least he could see that.

Kathryn furrowed her brow, but she wasn't glaring anymore. "The *entire* forest?"

Dylan nodded. "I'm also not a very bright barbarian." His intelligence was five. "Me check for trap. Keep safe," he said in a booming baritone.

Sydney giggled, and Trevor rolled his eyes. Everyone watched Dylan with either curiosity or amusement. Perfect.

Sydney rolled the dice and stared at Dylan, mouth slightly open, when it came up twenty.

She rolled again. Another twenty.

One more time, and this time it came back a one.

She puffed out her cheeks and blew out a long breath. "Okay. You may not be the brightest or most observant barbarian ever, but you do have a fighter's instinct and an intense love of gold. Something calls to you from the middle of the forest. The ancient lessons of your ancestors say it's probably gold. Or a dragon. Or a dragon protecting gold. Any of the above would pretty much make your month."

"Let's keep pushing into the forest." All of Kathryn's antipathy was gone.

"Agreed." Josh sat straighter, and his scowl vanished. "Are we rested enough to continue?"

Evan looked between them. "We should be good for a couple more hours. Are we certain?"

"*Yes,*" Josh and Kathryn spoke in unison.

Dylan just wanted to make everyone laugh a little. He hadn't expected an instant one-eighty in their attitudes. What had them so eager to push ahead where they hadn't agreed before?

"How close is this dragon?" Trevor's shoulders relaxed, and he leaned in, elbows on his knees.

"He's in the forest." Sydney looked like she was fighting a smile.

So worth it.

Evan drummed his fingers on his knee. Whatever Kathryn and Josh knew, her guys didn't seem to. "If I check for traps, will I find him?" Evan sounded doubtful.

"You can try, but he's not a trap." Sydney was definitely enjoying this.

Josh laughed. "Because your barbarian is so dumb, he doesn't know the difference."

"Guilty as charged." Dylan knew the teasing was

friendly, and Sydney's pleased look was worth anything that came next.

"Okay," Evan said. "The barbarian takes the lead. He can follow his *ancestral instinct* and be the front line if anything ambushes us. Kathryn can watch our rear."

Josh quirked an eyebrow. "So, same as always."

Kathryn blushed. "It's a good view."

"Do you want to do any more prep before you go in?" Sydney asked.

Dylan's character might be stupid, but he wasn't *that* into the role playing. "Yes."

"No." Josh and Kathryn were in agreement again.

Sydney looked at Evan and Trevor, who shrugged.

"Apparently they know something we don't," Trevor said. "We side with the sexy monk."

Dylan knew when he was outvoted, and his curiosity was screaming for answers. "I'm in. Let's go."

19

They wandered for what Sydney said was a couple miles, with Dylan in the lead. The sun was setting, and the longer they traveled, the harder it was to see their path.

And then a light broke through the trees. Dylan led them toward the glow. The group reached a clearing and squinted in the brightness.

Dylan was as on edge as Trevor and Even, as they waited for their eyes to adjust.

Kathryn and Josh were already striding forward.

"There's a building in the clearing that looks like a Disney castle," Sydney said. "Spires stretching toward the sky, and opaque crystal walls glinting at you. You've never seen a building so stunning or so completely impractical.

"A woman strolls around the corner. She's tall and slender, and it's difficult for you to determine her age. When you look closer, if you squint, her form seems to shimmer and fade, and you see the hulking shape of a grand dragon wrapped around the building, its scales the same color as her vibrant leather outfit."

It sounded stunning, but Dylan didn't see why this was enough to make Josh and Kathryn get along.

Josh looked like he was fighting a smirk. "I stroll forward and bow. Great and mighty goddess, we're here out of respect, and not to intrude."

"I join him." Kathryn nudged Evan and Trevor. "We all do. Thank you for gracing us with your presence, Mistress."

"Me too?" Dylan was almost bursting from curiosity.

Sydney's smile was mischievous. "Inside my home are wonders from around the universe. Technology, knowledge, weapons… Treasures you've only imagined. To gain access, you must each complete a quest. Because you're a group, if every single one of you doesn't pass your individual quest, you won't be allowed inside."

That sounded… vague. "What kind of a quest?" Dylan asked.

"It will vary from person to person." Sydney rattled the dice in her hand. She rolled. "And your mage goes first."

"I didn't agree to this." Trevor held up his hands.

Kathryn gave him a sweet, wide-eyed stare. "Please?"

"All right." Trevor's sigh was exaggerated. "What's my quest?"

Sydney rolled again, then checked something on her phone. "You have to sing us the song of your choice."

"What?" His tone went flat. "Why would I do that? What's inside that's so great? Are all the quests like this?"

"Do you forfeit?" Sydney studied him. "Because you cost your entire party if you do."

He looked at Kathryn. "You have some idea what's in there. What's so great that you're dying to do this?"

Dude was kind of a whiny dick.

She pursed her lips. "We don't know until we go inside."

"Of course she has an idea," Josh said. "But if you're not going to play, why are you here?"

Evan clenched his fist and glared at Josh.

Kathryn rested a hand on Evan's leg, but her attention was on Trevor. "Play the fucking game, please?" Her voice was sugary sweet.

Dylan wasn't sure how he felt about her boyfriends, but he could see why she and Sydney were close friends. Kind until the situation called for otherwise, and then the sweetness faded.

"We all have to do something similar." Josh's good mood was fading too. "Are you a coward?"

Trevor raised an eyebrow. "Are you the kind of asshole who thinks he can goad me into something by calling me names?"

"Are you done being contrary?" Evan asked.

Trevor shrugged. "I guess. It's roleplaying, right?"

Dylan doubted that was the real reason for the attitude. He was tempted to deck the guy.

"The dragon wants to know what song you choose, and if you'd like accompanying music," Sydney said.

Trevor shook his head. "I've got this. The song is a surprise."

He sang "Don't Stop Believin'" by Journey. It was acapella and amazing. Dude had an incredible voice.

Now Dylan really wanted to deck him.

Until Sydney clapped, glee on her face. It was worth the headache. "Your barbarian is next," she said.

And Dylan was going to do whatever it was he was asked, without argument, because doing otherwise was ridiculous. No one could follow an act like Trevor's anyway.

"You have to tell a joke," Sydney said.

He stared at her in disbelief. "A… what now?"

Kathryn let out a low growl.

Josh clenched his jaw.

"A joke. Tell a joke. That's your quest." Sydney didn't look fazed.

If he was going to do it, he might as well get it over with. "Uh…" His mind was a blank. He'd heard hundreds of jokes in his life, and some were even funny. It figured that only one came to mind now. Well, aside from a punchline he never remembered the beginning of. *You think I asked for a twelve-inch pianist?*

He sighed. "What did Cinderella say when she got to the ball?"

"What?" Sydney raised an eyebrow.

"Nothing. She just gagged a little."

Everyone groaned, except for Josh, who snorted with a tiny laugh. Thank God for him.

"I don't think that counts," Evan said.

Sydney fixed her gaze on him. "The dragon hears your complaint and wonders why you're making this more difficult for your own party. The dragon would also like to point out the requirement wasn't to tell a *funny* joke, and that you were trying not to laugh despite your protests. And by the way, you're next."

Evan had to recite a line from his favorite movie… in character. He did a fantastic Casper Van Diem impersonation, though Dylan wasn't sure how he felt about anyone calling *Starship Troopers* their favorite movie.

Kathryn had to dance. If Dylan had landed on that one after that stripper routine last weekend, he probably would have made Sydney prove that was really what he'd rolled.

There was a fluidity in Kathryn's movements that reflected her skill with Aikido. It wasn't a stunning ballet, but it was amazing to watch.

Dylan had been wrong. She definitely followed up Trevor's act, and blew it out of the water.

And then it was Josh's turn.

Sydney scrunched up her face as she stared at the dice. "Apparently, you've picked the wildcard."

"What does that mean?" Dylan asked. He could see why Kathryn and Josh wanted to visit the dragon. This was ridiculous, but it was fun. With Trevor's tantrum out of the way, the mood in the room was lighter.

"It's quester's choice… sort of," Sydney explained. "He has to pick from one of the tasks someone who came before him already performed."

Josh twisted his face in consideration. "What if I pick nothing?"

Sydney looked amused. "Then the dragon will get angry, point out you know that's not how this works, and eat you before letting the rest of your party in."

"I'll die?"

"If you're lucky." There was no irritation in Sydney's voice. Her smile never faded.

Josh looked around the room. "What should I pick?"

Everyone had a slightly different opinion.

Josh stood, stretched his arms over his head, and rolled his neck. "I pick the dance." He extended his arm toward Sydney. "But only if the dragon dances with me."

She shook her head and pushed his hand away. "The dragon doesn't dance."

Dylan had the feeling this particular quest hadn't come up before.

"Maybe the dragon shouldn't hand out quests she's not willing to complete herself," Josh teased.

Her smile grew. She grasped his fingers, and he tugged her to her feet. A few swipes on his phone, and a tinny dance beat filtered into the room.

Where Kathryn was like liquid given life, Josh was something rougher. He was just as graceful, but it was fucking dirty. Grinding, groping, and on top of it all, correcting for any misstep Sydney made, so she was part of the entire thing.

Dylan's skin hummed, heat pouring through his veins, as he watched the two of them. There was no jealousy. Only the desire to not have three other people in the room.

Trevor cleared his throat. "Will the healer be fucking the dragon in front of us, or can we see what this is all about now?" His tone was light and playful.

Sydney's skin darkened. Josh spun her one more time and held her hand until she was seated again, before returning to his own chair.

"The dragon is pleased. And appropriately humbled. She lets you in the building." Sydney was almost glowing. *That* was magic. "It's a library and a museum all in one. Vast and glorious, and literally encompasses anything you can imagine. You're allowed to explore anywhere. There are rooms set aside for you to stay the night and rest in. When you're ready to continue your journey, you'll be given access to the armory, where you'll each receive a weapon or other gift, suited to your journey."

Evan's face lit up. "Can we go there first?"

"You can," Sydney said. "But remember, when you step through that door, your time here is done. You'll collect your reward, and be transported to another plane. So don't do it unless you're ready to leave."

They played for several hours, and the mood stayed light. They ordered pizza in the afternoon, and stayed immersed in the game until almost midnight, when Kathryn announced she had a morning class and really needed to leave.

Dylan didn't remember the last time he'd had this kind of silly, careless, incredible fun, playing a game.

"Should we do this again next weekend?" Kathryn asked.

He was ready to say *of course,* when he saw the whisper of a frown cross Sydney's face.

ONLY ONE THING WAS MAKING SYDNEY HESITATE TO answer Kathryn's question. A *yes* was more than the start of a new gaming schedule with friends. If she kept hanging out with Josh like this, she wouldn't be able to ignore the pull. This was more than friendship. She didn't know why she'd thought she could pretend otherwise.

She landed on, "Probably. I'll let you know."

"Perfect."

Kathryn and her boyfriends said *goodbye* and were on their way.

Dylan closed the door behind them and turned back to Sydney. "Why did you hesitate?"

Of course he had to ask her that. She couldn't keep this in her head. It was the kind of decision she didn't get to make on her own. She knew how she felt, but that didn't mean Dylan would agree.

Or Josh.

Did she want to have this conversation with both of them at the same time?

That made more sense than not. The way they both stared at her made her brain stall.

"I can go wait in my room, if you need to discuss this." A whisper of hurt lined Josh's voice.

Sydney didn't blame him. She didn't want him to be here as just a back-up penis. She wanted…

She wanted what Kathryn had. It wasn't that easy, though. All of this was lessening the ache of why she and Josh broke up, but it wasn't erasing the memory.

And they were still staring at her.

"I don't have a problem with you saying whatever's on your mind in front of both of us," Dylan said. "There are so many blurred lines here, it would be nice to erase a few and draw new ones. Maybe… more inclusive ones."

Sydney summoned her courage—the words weren't forming, so hopefully this would work as an alternative—and looked at Josh. "I know you're sick of hearing this, but I still have doubts. You hurt me.

When you say you won't do it again, you believe it. But I need to as well…" She bit her bottom lip. This wasn't what she wanted to say, but it was too late to change course. "I'd rather stop looking over my shoulder, waiting for a fuck up to happen."

"That does make friendship easier." Dylan's tone was impossible to decipher.

She didn't know Dylan well. They had fun together. He'd proven over and over that he was sincere, and the only time he'd let her down was with that damn blind spot he had for Josh. Which—Sydney had one too.

"What if we tried what Kathryn, Trevor, and Evan are doing?" That was both easier and far harder to say than she expected.

She swore her heart stopped when Dylan raised his eyebrows.

She didn't know to interpret that. *Please, don't let this be a mistake*. "What if all three of us were dating?"

"Why did you phrase it that way?" Josh asked.

She shook her head. "I don't understand."

"You didn't ask about us dating you. You said *all three of us*."

"The two of you are more than friends." She couldn't ignore it. She didn't want to. "It doesn't matter what you tell me or yourselves."

"We're not…" Dylan trailed off.

Josh gave a scoffing laugh. "Aren't we?"

This entire idea terrified Sydney, but now that she'd said it aloud, it also raced over her with sparks of anticipation. There were so many places things could go wrong. Josh and Dylan could decide they only wanted each other. Josh could make the same mistakes he had before. She and Dylan might realize they didn't like each other as they spent more time together.

And at this moment, it all seemed worth it. Heartbreak would tear her apart—she already felt it—but if everything went right…

"Yeah, we are more than friends." When Dylan spoke, Sydney's breath hitched.

He crossed the distance to Josh in a few short strides, grabbed a fistful of Josh's shirt, and crushed their mouths together.

Sydney bit the inside of her cheek, and heat spilled through her at the intense affection they radiated. It was so obvious they cared for each other.

She didn't want to interrupt, but she did want to get in on the kissing. The push and pull between Dylan and Josh sang in her veins and danced on the tip of her tongue.

When Josh looked at her, the desire in his gaze clenched around her heart. He gripped her wrist tight and tugged her close. A sliver of apprehensive mingled with her desire.

She needed to give him enough trust to make this work. Not all of it. Not yet.

Who was she kidding? Regardless of what she told herself, her heart was already going to shatter if things went south again.

Might as well enjoy the ride.

The way he kissed her, hard and hungrily, teeth nipping her lips, made it easy to shove her doubt into a box and lock it in the back of her mind. God, she'd missed this with Josh. His mouth on her skin numbed the ache of longing that pinged behind her ribs.

He kneaded her breast through her shirt. She loved the rough intensity in each touch. The need. The frantic groping. She melted into him, wanting to be as close as possible, and his erection dug into her stomach.

This was what the dance earlier promised, but couldn't deliver on with an audience. This time, they didn't have to stop.

"This is better than watching the two of you dance." Dylan's words echoed her thoughts. He kissed along the back of her neck and shoved her shirt up, sliding his palms along her bare skin.

Sydney reached back to feel more of him, and he pressed into her touch, his cock jerking though his jeans against her hand.

Being the filling in this sandwich was becoming one of her favorite things.

Josh spun her away, startling her, and dragged his hands down her arms to capture her wrists, before she could question him.

She tugged, and he gripped her tighter. The resistance made her smile.

He nipped her earlobe, his breath hot on her skin. "You got to call the shots before. Our turn now."

Her pulse screamed through her veins with anticipation, and her heart hammered against her ribs. His throaty promise combined with the way Dylan studied her, like she was lunch, made her squirm in the best possible way.

Dylan undid her jeans, and tugged them and her panties down to her knees.

Apparently it *was* possible to crank her anticipation higher, because every time he did this, something delicious came next. And then so did she.

He knelt in front of her, and she whimpered before he even touched her skin. He kissed along her bare hip, her stomach, the top of her thigh.

When Dylan licked along her slit, she groaned and pressed into his face. Josh kept her from moving more, which increased her desire with each new swipe of Dylan's tongue.

He wrapped his lips around her clit, and sucked.

Her gasps grew louder, and the thrust of her hips more frantic, as he alternated touches.

She clenched her fists and toes when she came, grinding into Dylan's face until it was too much, then jerking away.

Dylan rose and leaned past her, sandwiching her again, while he kissed Josh.

Her body heated to flaming at them sharing her

taste. She didn't know which of the three of them was moaning louder, but it was an amazing chorus.

Josh and Dylan broke apart, and Josh spun her back to him again. She'd worry about all of it making her dizzy, but the two men already had her head twisted and fuzzed in the best possible way.

"I don't like not being able to touch you." Josh stripped her shirt off, then kissed her. "I love seeing your gorgeous body," he shoved her pants the rest of the way off, "but hate holding myself back." He dragged his fingers up her back, pulling her into him. "Now that I have you again, you should know I don't ever plan to let you go."

His words and the way he held her tight spilled through her with love, but a whisper of fear. If she wasn't careful, she could fall into this and forget the last three years never happened. That they'd never been apart.

Was that a good thing or a bad one?

"Come here." Josh grasped her fingers, and led her into the bedroom.

She heard Dylan follow. She trusted him to join in or watch as he wanted.

And she was so wrapped up in Josh right now, it was scary.

He stripped out of his clothes, claiming a kiss between each discarded article, then scooted onto the bed and pulled her with him. "I want to watch you ride me," he said. "I want to see as much of you as possible as I slide inside you. When you come."

Sydney didn't have a witty response, or any at all beyond straddling his legs. He skated his palms up her thighs. The way he raked his gaze over her, she felt like the most beautiful woman in the world.

She tried to tease, hovering over him, the head of his cock nudging her opening.

He gripped her thighs, and laughed through clenched teeth. "We have so much time to play. Later." He thrust up, filling her up and spreading her open. "I've waited too long to feel you wrapped around me, knowing it would last."

Sydney lowered herself onto him, sighing with pleasure as he was buried himself inside her.

He set a slow, even pace, rocking against her. Holding her gaze with his own.

The mattress shifted with a new weight, and Dylan knelt next to Sydney. He'd shed his clothing as well, and his cock stood at attention. He crushed his mouth to hers while he covered her hand and lowered it to his shaft.

Sydney didn't need to be prompted twice. She stroked Dylan's hard length while she moaned into his kisses. Josh slid inside her, hammering harder and faster with each passing moment.

Dylan dragged a thumb over one of her nipples, and she gasped. She didn't know which way to turn, to enjoy ever touch. She tumbled into the blend of it all. Josh pounding against her. Dylan teasing and kissing her.

When Josh pressed his thumb to her clit, she

whimpered. He stroked the still-tender nub, coaxing her toward another climax.

She lost track of who was doing what. All she knew was it was so much *everything*. She hovered near orgasm, falling into a delicious haze when Dylan pinched her nipple and rolled it between his fingers.

She screamed when she came, clenching hard around Josh, forgetting for a moment that she still gripped Dylan.

As the edge softened, her desire lingered. She resumed stroking Dylan, keeping time with Josh's thrusts.

Their grunts and groans were musical. Dylan's grip on her breast tightened, and his breathing grew more shallow. She squeezed just a little with each stroke.

He came hard, coating her hand, her thighs, and Josh's stomach.

Josh gripped her thighs tighter. He was close too. He hammered against her, skin slapping skin, squeezing her legs as he spilled inside her.

Everything slowed, except for the euphoria filling Sydney's head. She could stay here forever, wrapped in this fantasy-come-to-life, pressed between two incredible men.

And as long as the post-coital giddiness lingered, she could ignore the nagging voice that insisted it was only matter of time before Josh fucked up again.

21

Josh was still buzzing from the weekend. It was like it used to be, but better. He was still having a little trouble believing it, but it had been incredible.

"Mr. Hunter. My office, now." His mother's sharp tone as she strolled by his desk caught him off guard.

Whatever she was upset about wasn't going to ruin his morning. He grabbed a pen and notepad and followed.

"What's wrong with you?" she asked the instant the door swung shut behind him. She set her coffee mug on her desk and her purse in its assigned drawer, never making eye contact.

"Do you want a list, or is there a specific offense I've committed?" He kept his tone light.

She unpacked her laptop and set it on its docking station. "Aaron forwarded me an email this morning.

A response to a *Cease and Desist* on the *Changelings and Caravans* game."

How did he have that already? Josh had only forwarded it to his friend yesterday. Actually, why did Aaron have that at all? Josh kept the question to himself. Admitting he knew anything was a confession of guilt. "Okay?"

"I've been reading your papers since you were old enough to write. I've read a number of your legal briefs and letters. Her *lawyer* is one of your frat brothers." She finally sat and fixed a glare on him.

All circumstantial evidence. But also, *fuck*. "And?"

"Are you an idiot? You can't do things like this." The tight edge that wove though her voice spoke to every time she'd lectured Josh throughout his life.

He wasn't letting it get to him, and he wasn't admitting guilt. "Like what?"

Laurie Hunter scrubbed her face. "I'm not in the mood to play games with you. Let's assume you're going to continue to deny this and that I'm going to continue to not believe your bullshit."

Lovely. Not. Then why pretend? "Why does Aaron have a response sent to someone who isn't related at all to this firm?"

"Our client is licensing rights to publish a product someone else is making a claim on. This has everything to do with us."

"It doesn't." Josh didn't like this. "Sydney is handling it. It's not a legitimate claim. Why does Aaron have that letter?"

"Even if you don't care how this reflects on our firm, she's dating your roommate. It's time to move on."

"Right." Josh should counter her complete and total deflection of his question, but she'd tripped him up. He hadn't considered the fallout of their relationship this weekend. If they kept going long term, all three of them, how was he supposed to explain it?

"*Right?* Is she or isn't she?"

"She definitely is. Dylan is absolutely devoted to Sydney."

"Good. Great. Let her ruin his life instead of yours."

Anger surged inside, white-hot and obliterating any reason in its path. "Excuse me?" He didn't know what made him more furious—the comment about Sydney, or the complete disregard for Dylan. "Sydney is talented and creative and brilliant, and Dylan is one of the best fucking junior attorneys you've ever had."

His mother's eyes narrowed. "And here's the problem. *You* should be one of the best I've ever had. But that *girl* got under your skin and fucked with your head. She almost talked you out of law school."

Josh didn't try to suppress his growl. "No. *I* almost talked me out of law school. I didn't know if I wanted to spend another three years in a classroom, for something I wasn't going to use."

"And she left, and you figured out you were wrong."

"I wasn't wrong. I just had the wrong goal in mind."

She twisted her mouth in that sideways irritated way that meant this argument would only get worse. "And what goal is that?"

Working here. "Did you know she was the other party in this negotiation?"

"Yes."

Josh clenched a fist. "Is that why you pulled me?"

Now his mother was smiling. That eerie, cold kind of smile that didn't reach his eyes. When he was younger, it would have chilled him. Now it cranked the heat another notch higher on his anger.

"I've done everything to prepare you for this job. And that includes keeping her out of your path," she said.

The late nights of work emergencies. The missed, super important dates. No. She couldn't mean that.

"You could have trusted me to decide on my own."

"Not if that decision included throwing away your future for something frivolous. I've done all of this for you. We're having this conversation for you. So that you don't destroy your legacy."

Josh had been hearing that all his life. He'd taken it to heart. Sydney's voice echoed in his thoughts—*For a job you don't even want.*

But he'd done what he was supposed to. Gone to law school. Passed his bar. Put in the hours. Surrendered the woman he loved…

Sydney was right. It was all for something he didn't want to be doing. Not here. Not like this. "No. This wasn't for me. It was all for you."

His mother's face contorted with rage, and her skin was blotched and red. "You ungrateful, selfish—"

"No. I'm not." He stood. "I appreciate everything you've given me, and I agonize over every single decision I know will disappoint you. I also don't work for you anymore. Consider this my resignation." His thoughts fluctuated between anger and apathy. He should be nervous or scared by what he was doing. Instead, calm was settling in. "And not that it's ever been your business, but I am seeing Sydney again. So's Dylan. And we're all okay with that."

An icy mask slid into place, more concerning that her fury. "Clean your desk and get the fuck out of my office. *Now*."

"Of course, Ms. Hunter. Have a lovely day." Josh didn't slam the door. He let it swing shut softly behind him as he strolled away.

He didn't know what to make of his thoughts… Which feeling to focus on. He could scream—at himself or his mother—or laugh at the sense of relief that threatened his thoughts. Cry. Curse three years in law school just to wind up here.

He swallowed it all for the moment. Any reaction would wait until he left the office.

Josh was shoving the last of his belongings into a box, when Dylan approached.

"What are you doing?" Dylan's voice was low.

Josh shrugged. Could he talk without unleashing the flood of confusion that roared inside? "What's it look like?"

Dylan furrowed his brow. He liked it here. There was no reason to drag him down.

"I'll text you." Josh grabbed his stuff and walked toward the stairs.

He was shaking by the time he slid into his car. The yell he expected to tear free wouldn't come. He pressed his forehead into the cool steering wheel and took several deep breaths.

The action didn't help him sort out his head, but it helped him unclench his fists.

Now what?

Go back upstairs and apologize? Beg for his job back? Reach out directly to the publisher and ask for a chance to work for them, despite the way he left his last job?

Start drinking at eight in the morning?

Josh didn't know. And the thing that scared him the most was he wasn't worried about it.

SYDNEY WAS DOING HER BEST NOT TO FIDGET, AS SHE waited to be shown into a conference room.

She shouldn't be as nervous as last time—Dylan and Josh went over the entire contract with her yesterday. Not that she'd tell anyone about their help. That wasn't a relationship line they'd completely obliterated.

None of what they told her was unexpected. The offer was an advance against royalties, to distribute her game. It was a good advance, too. Enough to keep her solvent for a couple of years, and hopefully give the game time to earn out, and maybe she could pitch them her next idea as well.

And this was the big day. She was surrendering some of her control to this publisher. It meant more money, more support, and with a little luck, more contracts in the future. It was still new and scary, though.

Sydney wanted to wander by Dylan's and Josh's desks while she waited. Say *hi*. Chat for a few minutes and maybe take her mind off the morning.

She wouldn't put them in that position. They'd be available after work.

"Ms. Brimhall? They're ready for you." A man about her age showed her back to the same conference room they'd been in before.

She resisted the urge to crane her neck for a glimpse of either of her guys.

Her guys. The phrase was enough to let a tiny smile poke through the tension. This weekend had been incredible. In some ways, she had a hard time believing it was real. If she could keep the memories hovering in her mind without blushing through this meeting, it would help her stay calm.

Dylan wasn't in here today. Not that she was surprised.

After a round of handshakes and polite conversation, they got down to business. Aaron Jorgensen handed her the contract and a pen, and asked if she had any final questions.

She tried to read everything though again, telling herself Aaron's fingers drumming on the table had nothing to do with her going slowly. Her eyes glazed over after two or three pages.

She settled for skimming the rest, mostly for show. It made her look more professional, didn't it?

And then it was over. Weeks of stress and worrying, just to be done with the final step in less than half an hour.

She shook everyone's hands again. Josh had told her that while it wasn't in the contract, and she didn't hear it from him, that she should drop the hint that she had more ideas.

She reached their art director. "I'm looking forward to discussing future ideas with you."

"That won't be necessary." His tone was cool, and his expression cold. "It was a pleasure meeting you."

Oh. Sydney's smile froze in place, and a response stuck in her throat. Was that a brush-off? From the company who was distributing her game?

"Thank you again for coming down here, Ms. Brimhall." Aaron showed her from the room and walked her to the elevator. "Have a wonderful day."

Why did she feel like she'd just been pushed aside

in a not-good way? Was the clenching in her gut the tail end of nerves?

She checked her messages as she rode the lift down to the parking garage. One from Dylan said *Congratulations*.

The other, from Josh, said, *Call me when you're done. We'll get late breakfast*.

Shouldn't he be working?

She settled into her car. The churning in her gut was worse now. Something was wrong. Josh would have to wait a few minutes.

She pulled the contract from her briefcase.

The first few pages were what she expected. And that eyes-glazing-over feeling was back. This time, she was reading the whole thing.

When she got to the section about rights, her gut sank. *Work for hire*. The phrase glared at her like it was written in neon. She read the section over and over. There was nothing in here about an advance. About royalties.

If she was reading this right, it said she's just surrendered her game and its characters in their entirety to the distributors.

This wasn't what she'd reviewed with Josh and Dylan. She had to be reading it wrong. She wouldn't have signed this. She'd turned down similar offers in the past.

It didn't matter how many times she read it. It still said *Work for hire*.

This was bullshit. Confusion and doubt gave way

to anger. They had her sign a different contract than the one she'd reviewed.

Sydney needed to undo this. She headed back upstairs.

"May I help you, Miss?" The same man who had shown her to her meeting was working the reception desk.

She'd be polite and cool about this. She wouldn't freak out without proof. "I think there's an issue with the contract I just signed. I'd like to speak to Aaron Jorgensen or someone else who can help me."

"I see. Are you a client?"

"No. But I was just here. You saw me."

He shook his head. "We can't offer legal advice to people who aren't our clients. I'm sorry. You'll need to speak with your own attorney."

"*My* attorney didn't prepare this contract." She struggled to keep her frustration from bleeding into something more intense. "I'd like to speak with the person who did."

"We don't do that. I'm sorry. You can have your lawyer schedule a time with someone here if there are concerns. We can't help you if you're not a client."

Was she not making herself clear? "This doesn't have anything to do with whether or not I pay someone here. I just want to speak with one of the people who prepared this contract." She could ask for Josh or Dylan, but she didn't want to get them in trouble.

"We can't help you." He turned back to his computer.

She slammed her palm on the reception counter. "Just let me talk to someone!" The shout came out without her permission, but she didn't want to take it back.

"You need to leave."

"You pulled a fucking bait and switch." Now that she was yelling, she couldn't stop. "I *need* to speak with someone here, or I'll sue your asses off." Which she couldn't even begin to afford, but it sounded good.

"Then your lawyer can call us." His voice wavered.

"Is there a problem, Ms. Brimhall?" Laurie Hunter's voice drew Sydney's attention. She stood a few feet away, watching Sydney with a venom-filled glare.

Sydney swallowed the impulse that was always there to cower in front of this woman. "This contract isn't the one I was given to review. It was swapped for a bullshit version I never would have signed if I'd known."

"Did you read this one before you signed it?"

Sydney clenched her jaw and struggled to ignore the embarrassed, awkward girl who wanted to emerge. "I glanced at it."

"Then you knew what it contained. We're not responsible for seller's remorse, especially when you're not our client. You need to leave."

"I just want you to hear me out." Sydney's retort came out as more of a plea than a demand.

Someone loosely grabbed her arm. A man in a security uniform had stepped up next to her. "Miss, please come with me."

Humiliation mingled with her fury. She wanted to break away and throw a tantrum until they listened. It wouldn't do her any good. "Fine. But we're not done."

"Yes we are, Sydney. Don't come back here. Next time, I'll call the police." A strong threat wove through Laurie's reply.

Sydney blinked back the tears that pricked her eyelids as she stepped onto the elevator for the five-billionth time that day, this time with Security by her side.

Josh wanted to meet up. He could help her figure this out.

Unless he was in on it.

She growled mentally at the doubt and refused to give it any attention.

Because you know it's possible.

No. She wasn't listening. La la la la.

They reached her car, and the security guy waited near the hood. Was he going to stand there until she left?

He crossed his arms.

Apparently so.

She was going to cry. And then be sick. And then cry some more.

22

It was rare for Dylan to be so distracted, it got in the way of what he should be doing. This morning though, he had zero focus.

Moments after Josh walked out of the office and left an empty desk behind, he sent a text. *I quit. My choice. I'll explain later. Don't let this fuck you too.*

Dylan asked for details.

Josh's response was, *Tell you at lunch. Best said in person.*

Not reassuring.

Dylan's level of distraction doubled when the clock ticked up toward Sydney's meeting. She'd be fine. Everything would go smoothly. It was a basic contract.

He forced his head down… and stared blankly at his screen.

Nope. Nothing was getting done today. At least not until he had some answers.

He sent Sydney a quick text that said *Congratulations*. That helped a little, even if she wouldn't see it or respond until she left.

A loud noise carried from the lobby, and Dylan frowned. Sydney?

No.

There was another yell.

That was definitely Sydney. He was halfway out of his chair, when Laurie Hunter paused in front of his desk.

Rage radiated from her. "I swear to God, if you go out there, you'll never practice law in this city."

He sank back into his seat as she stalked away. Was she serious?

Did it matter, if something was wrong with Sydney?

He didn't know what was happening. Was he willing to risk Laurie's threat being real if this was something he shouldn't be involved in?

It was Sydney. If he could help, he would. If not, he'd be there for her.

At the cost of his career?

He was on his feet before the question finished scrolling through his thoughts.

When he reached the lobby, Sydney was stepping into the elevator with Security. She didn't look up before the doors closed.

What the fuck?

He whirled to face Laurie. Red splotches dotted

her face, and she was watching him with poison in her eyes.

Well, *fuck*.

She closed her eyes, and her chest rose and fell. When she met his gaze again, her mask was back in place.

This was honestly more terrifying than her fury. It didn't matter. He was ready to run downstairs, to stop Sydney.

"Take the rest of the day off," Laurie said in a cool tone. "I'm giving you permission, because you're going to do it anyway."

He was sprinting toward the stairs before she finished speaking. Her words hit his back as the stairwell door closed behind him, and he wasn't sure he heard her right.

"Tell my son I'm sorry."

That couldn't be what she said. She never referred to Josh as her son in the office. And she *never* apologized once she'd taken a stand.

He'd deal with it later. As he reached the parking garage, the security guy who'd escorted Sydney out was heading back to the elevators.

"Where is she parked?" Dylan asked.

"The chubby girl? She's gone. Watched her leave."

Dylan clenched his fist. It was so tempting to deck the guy for the *chubby* comment. But there were more important things to deal with. Like finding out *what the fuck was going on*.

He needed to grab his stuff from his desk. On the

trip up, he sent Josh and Sydney both texts that said he'd be at the coffee shop a block from the office, and that he'd wait for the next hour, unless they said they weren't coming.

Already there. Josh's reply came before Dylan was back on the ground floor.

There was no response from Sydney.

Dylan was both grateful for the short stroll to the coffee shop, and irritated it took so long to get there. By the time he walked in the front door, adrenaline hammered full force in his veins, and his body was wound tighter than a spring.

He didn't have to look, to know Josh would be at the same table they always sat at. He crossed the room without pausing, bent at the waist, and kissed Josh hard, pouring several hours of built-up tension into the connection.

This was the one thing that felt right about the morning. Like it should have been this way long ago.

When Dylan broke away, Josh wore a faint smile, but it didn't erase the lines etched in his forehead.

Josh nodded at the seat across from him, and the second cup on the table. "Got you a drink. Decaf."

"Probably smart." Dylan would have scoffed at the idea on any other day. He sipped the still-scalding coffee. Should he ask what happened to Josh first, or tell him about Sydney? He knew which he'd want to hear, if he was the guy with half the information—the other half.

"Why aren't you at work?" Josh asked.

"Your mom gave me the day off. I think between you quitting and Security escorting Sydney from the build—"

"What?"

Dylan shrugged. "I don't know much. There was yelling—Sydney's—and when I got out to the lobby, they were seeing her to her car. And then she was gone."

"Fucking… I'd say *unbelievable,* but let me guess. My mother was involved." Josh's laugh was bitter.

"She looked worse than I've ever seen her. Laurie did. Not just angry, but… stressed."

Josh's scowl wavered. "She brought it on herself."

"What happened?"

"I don't even know where to start." Josh sighed through his fingers as he rubbed his face. "She knew I drafted that letter for Sydney. She told me Sydney was going to ruin your career and better you than me. She implied pretty heavily that she'd worked hard to keep me away from Sydney…"

There was so much to unpack there, Dylan didn't know where to start. "And then you quit."

"Wouldn't you?"

Dylan's decision wouldn't be as straightforward as Josh's. He liked his job. Then again, he'd been willing to be fired less than an hour ago. "I don't blame you."

"I don't know what to do." Josh slumped in his chair. "I can't believe… The only part of this not devouring me is the actual quitting. Fuck, that felt good. Why hasn't Tink replied to my messages?"

Dylan had a similar concern. "I told her the same thing I said to you—that I'd be here for an hour." Did they wait here or try to track her down? See if she was at her apartment, or… Dylan didn't know where else they'd look.

But he was worried about her.

Sydney got Dylan's message before she was more than a few blocks from the law offices. She'd wavered about going to meet him. He could explain. Help her understand.

Or he could ask her what the fuck her problem was, and chide her for acting so unprofessionally in the place he worked.

No. That wasn't Dylan.

It was Josh.

He'd said he was sorry.

Less than two weeks after he'd pulled the same shit as when they were dating—picking work over her.

His apology was like every other time.

Dylan meant it, though. He was so close to perfect. Doting. Sweet. Understanding. Sexy as fuck.

Too perfect?

She let out a wordless scream in the car. It didn't silence the gnawing argument in her head.

Sydney headed home, instead of replying. She needed to get herself under control. There was a freak-out crawling under her skin. The kind of insecurity she could usually suppress with a few distractions.

Today it roared for her attention. When she got home, she shed her professional outfit, not caring where they landed, and yanked on her baggiest, most comfortable clothes. The sweats and T-shirt she'd lived in for a week after she broke up with Josh.

Was she an idiot? Was this all a joke on their part?

No. It was too elaborate for that. It was a misunderstanding. For some reason they'd gone over a different version of the contract with her than she was handed today. It wasn't their fault.

Unless it was.

No. She couldn't listen to that voice. She'd call them. Call Dylan. Even when they fought, he was honest with her.

Unless he's been making fun of you this entire time and you didn't see it.

She pressed her palm to her forehead, to squash the doubt.

Ignoring your instinct won't make it any less true.

No. Nononono.

Her phone buzzed with two messages. Identical, from Josh and Dylan.

Worried about you. Leaving here in 15. Coming to find you.

Because they cared. Because they could make this right.

Because they want to poke fun at the fat girl who thought two sexy as fuck men not only liked her, but were willing to share. Who does that?

She sobbed and knotted her fingers in her hair, yanking until her skull ached.

You can't ignore this. Deal with it now, and it will hurt less.

It wasn't true. Dylan hadn't… Neither had Josh. That wasn't who they were.

You don't know Dylan. Except that he's been fucking Josh for the last three years.

That didn't matter. It might to some people. She was not only fine with it, she was great with it. They were happy together.

Without you.

No. She wanted to scream again, but would it do her any good?

"Sydney?" Dylan's muffled voice carried through the front door, followed by a knock.

She clenched her jaw, to hold back the surge of doubt-induced nausea.

"We want to know what happened," Josh said.

Because they cared.

Because the joke isn't done.

She wasn't listening to that voice. It was a liar and an asshole.

You're going to let them in, looking like this?

She smoothed her hair the best she could, ignored the question, and went to open the door.

Dylan's expression softened when he saw her. "Fuck, Syd. What happened?" He reached toward her.

She stepped away instinctively.

Hurt splashed across his face. Or a scowl.

He's upset that you're not playing along.

She hated herself when she got like this. Then again, that was the point.

"Can we come in?" Josh asked.

She was too frazzled to do anything besides open the door wider and step aside.

"Did you come here to reinforce Laurie's threat?" Sydney's question came out raw.

Josh frowned. "She threatened you?"

Maybe they didn't know what happened.

Of course they know.

She clenched her fist until her nails dug into her palm. "She told me if I ever stepped foot in your law offices again, she'd have me arrested."

"What? Why?" Dylan's shock looked genuine.

Sydney wanted to believe it was. "Do you really not know?"

"I quit before your appointment. I wasn't in the office. Dylan only heard the shouting." Josh stepped closer. He flexed his fingers.

She wanted to fall into comfort from both of them. It was so tempting. They could tell her this was all a big mistake.

They could lie.

She forced steel through her veins and grabbed her copy of the contract from the briefcase she'd discarded by the door. "Read the section about rights and compensation. It's not what we talked about yesterday."

Dylan grabbed the paperwork, and Josh read over his shoulder.

Their frowns deepened, and silence stretched through the room, until Sydney couldn't ignore the ringing in her ears.

They didn't expect you to catch it so soon.

They didn't know it was there, or they would have told her.

You should have read before you signed. What were you thinking?

That regardless of what she thought of Laurie Hunter, the woman ran a solid and reputable firm.

Either that's not true, or you're just stupid.

Sydney tried to yank herself away from the hole she was plummeting into.

Dylan finally looked up. "This isn't the contract you were supposed to have."

"I figured that out. Thanks." She couldn't keep the sarcasm from her voice.

He thinks you're stupid.

Shut. Up.

Josh flipped to the last page. "But you signed it."

"Figured that out too. We're all on the same page now?"

"This isn't right." Dylan alternated his gaze between her and the contract. "Did Aaron tell you changes had been made?"

"Yeah. And I signed my life's work away anyway." Bitter sarcasm oozed from her reply. "No, he didn't fucking tell me. No one did."

"Well make this right," Josh said.

Don't say it. Don't say it. Don't say it.

Say it.

"Was this all fun and games for the two of you?" She hated herself even more when the words slipped out. "Fucking with my head? Making me think I was special? If you wanted to fuck me without lube, there were other ways to go about it."

Anger splashed across Dylan's face. "We didn't know about this."

"Yeah. Okay. You just happened to run into me right before this negotiation. You just happened to not know who I was. You just happened to be willing to give me all sorts of free legal advice. That just happened to be a completely and total *fucking lie*."

"That's not how it went down." Dylan's tone was turning hard. "I've always been sincere with you."

Bullshit.

Sydney didn't know anymore. She couldn't tell which of her thoughts hated her and which wanted what was best for her. Her chest ached, and her eyes ached, and her heart ached. "You need to leave."

"If that's what you want," Dylan said.

Of course he caved that easily. Because the game is over. He never cared.

Josh shook his head. "We're not going."

"*Get out.*" Sydney screamed so loudly, her voice cracked.

Josh didn't move, and he wasn't going to let Dylan go either. He'd seen this Sydney before, and a fist clenched around his lungs, squeezing his breath out, that she was falling into this.

The doubt. The disbelief. The years of external pressure, telling her so many things that weren't true. They'd worked through it when he and she first dated. He knew better than to ignore it or to walk away from her when she was like this, and he remembered how much it tore her apart both during and after.

Any other time she asked him to go, he would. This had to be the exception. "We're not leaving."

"Now." She spoke through clenched teeth.

"No." Dylan stood by his side.

Josh was a little surprised by that. Dylan didn't do complicated or drama. But Sydney was different.

Josh itched to reach out to her, but he wouldn't do

that yet. She needed to believe his sincerity first. "We're staying until you feel better," he said.

"Why?" Her question came out in a choked sob.

"I can only speak for me. I'm staying because I love you. I'm not making that up. I'm not saying that to poke fun at you. I love you so much. I've never stopped." He poured his heart into the words. This was one of those things he should always mean, and he'd done a shitty job of showing it in the past. "I was wrong back then, to set you aside the way I did. You mean so much more to me than that. I took us for granted, and you deserved better. You still do."

Her eyes glistened, and she scrubbed a hand across her cheeks.

He wasn't done yet. Now that the words were flowing, he couldn't dam up three years' worth of regret and missed opportunities. "When I tell you you're stunning, I mean it. Gorgeous eyes. Amazing body. Beautiful mind. Enviable, fuckable brain."

"Liar." Her protest was weak.

"Whatever your mind is telling you right now, it's the one lying." He didn't know if it would work, to be this direct. It might backfire on him. She might not be in the mood to hear it.

"Takes one to know one."

"I broke so many promises," Josh said. "I'm sorry. It was never because of you. What you and I had was incredible. The best thing ever, and I surrendered it. I was wrong."

"Please stop." She was begging now. "Don't make this worse."

This time he reached for her, placing a finger under her chin to look her in the eye. "Sydney, I mean everything I'm saying. I'll repeat it from now until eternity if that's what it takes to make you believe it. I love you more than anything—besides Dylan, but there's no competition there—you have a special place in my heart that no one else will ever fill. Whatever this is that you're feeling, whatever happened today, we'll plow our way through it. I'm on your side. I don't care what *Ms. Hunter* has to say. We'll make this right."

She stared back, eyes filled with unshed tears.

He was out of words, but he'd start over.

"I signed the contract." When she finally spoke, he let out a breath. "I didn't even read it. I trusted you both that it was what you said, and it wasn't. I walked in there this morning and signed my game away. I'm such a fucking idiot. I thought…"

Josh wasn't going to let her finish the thought, because that was the tip of the slide. He brushed his lips over hers and pulled back to meet her gaze again. "We didn't know. I swear to you. This is all wrong. Everything about the contract. But it doesn't have anything to do with how I feel about you."

"Same for me." Dylan spoke up. "This doesn't change my feelings at all. I mean everything I've always said. You're not a joke. You're… amazing."

Josh glided his hand down Sydney's arm, to grip

her fingers. He tugged her closer and brushed a strand of hair behind her ear. "You're not stupid. This isn't your fault. And we weren't involved."

"I don't..." She sighed. "I don't know anymore."

"I do. And you don't have to come up with answers right now. You need to pause. And think. And probably eat. You skipped breakfast, didn't you?"

She ducked her head. "I was too nervous."

"Come on." He tugged her into the kitchen, pulled out a chair, and nudged her into it. He knelt at her feet and kissed her knuckles. "One thing at a time. There's no reason to force any more than that."

"I guess." Most of the waver was gone from her reply, and exhaustion had moved in.

Every inch of him pleaded to wrap her up and hold her. Not until she was ready, though.

DYLAN WASN'T CERTAIN WHAT HE'D JUST SEEN, BUT HE had some assumptions that felt pretty right.

There was one thing he was sure of—Josh and Sydney may think they broke up, but it was more like a three-year hiatus. Whatever flowed between them in her living room, while she stood on the ledge of doubt and Josh talked her down, was more real and sincere than anything Dylan had ever seen.

When she'd started screaming without giving

them a chance to explain, instinct told Dylan to walk away.

The only desire he had with Sydney was to stay, though. It was equal parts because he cared, and because she was right to be furious. She'd just gotten fucked over hard.

Josh moved around the kitchen like it was his own. Knowing which cupboard the bowls were in. Where the spoons were. Where to look for the cereal.

They ate Corn Flakes in silence, with Sydney so drawn into herself, she looked like she wanted to hide in that oversized shirt.

Dylan could only guess at the rules of this, but the quiet didn't sit well with him. "This wasn't an honest mistake."

Sydney looked up from her food, eyes wide. Was she startled that he'd spoken or by what he said? She swallowed. "What do you mean?"

"Aaron Jorgensen is an incompetent asshole. We cover for him… always. Because he's sleeping with the boss." Dylan knew that didn't answer the question, but he was still sorting out his reasons for the declaration.

Sydney looked between them. "So the whole extreme-anti-nepotism thing stops at blood relatives?"

"Yup." Josh sighed. "But what Dylan's talking about… If Aaron did this, he'll be disbarred. He'll be shunned. This is career-ending shit."

Pieces were clicking in Dylan's head. "Only if he

gets caught. What was wrong with that last contract we fixed for him?"

"Everything was out of order. The formatting was screwed up." Josh pushed away his empty bowl. "Do you think… Was he doing the same thing there?"

It was a big assumption to make. Dylan couldn't proclaim Aaron was fucking with contracts without proof. But he and Josh helped implement the current document management system. Could they find proof? "Maybe. If he did this on purpose with Sydney, it can't be the first time. He didn't wake up this morning and think, *I'm going to cheat the system for this single client.*"

"He might have." Sydney didn't sound as pained as she had even a few minutes ago.

Dylan gave her a half-smile. "It's possible. But I don't think you're the only victim here."

"If you're saying that to make me feel better, it's working." Some of the tightness in her face melted away. "But someone would catch him, right? You said disbarment. What's worth that kind of risk?"

"Typically money." Josh cleared away their dishes, rinsed them, and set them in the sink.

How perfectly domestic was this, in the midst of this fucked-up day? Dylan didn't want to linger on it, but the simple actions left a warm glow inside, where he expected jealousy.

"How do you prove it? How can I help? Can I get my game back? Can I…" Sydney's scowl was back. "How can I help?"

What else was she about to say? "I can go in the system and compare changes. You two can't. Non-disclosure and all that."

"Okay, so… while it seems like a weird time to start caring about that *conflict of interest* line, I also understand this is more than a little bit of on-the-side legal advice," Sydney said. "But why can't Josh help you?"

Josh leaned against the counter near the sink. "Like I said. I quit this morning."

"Why?" Sydney asked.

"Because…" He raked his fingers through his hair. "Because I've never liked working there. And because I choose you."

"Oh." Sydney puffed out the reply on a soft sigh.

It was certainly one way to drive home the *I'm sorry, and here's proof I'll never do it again* point. Dylan couldn't argue with Josh's logic.

"There is something you can do." Dylan wanted to get to the bottom of this. He also needed to make sense of his own feelings. Whatever was happening between the three of them was more than just a casual hookup. It wasn't a simple *let's all date and see where it goes.* Something changed this morning, and he had to process.

Sydney leaned in. "Tell me. I can't… Sitting here, wallowing, will drive me insane."

"If Jorgensen has done this before, it's probably been in other cases like yours. People who came in without their own attorney. Smaller companies or individuals who couldn't afford to fight. And someone has probably bitched about it online."

"You want us to go play on the internet while you compare documents? That sounds grueling for you."

"It's not." Josh kicked away from the counter. "The system does ninety-nine percent of his work for him. We have to sift through search engines and blog posts and Reddit forums for our answers. And if we find proof, we have to hope my mother is willing to listen."

Dylan didn't want to doubt that part of the plan, but their past history of complaints about Aaron spoke for itself. This needed to not be for nothing.

And he had to figure out how to give Sydney the next bit of bad news. Best case scenario here was the publisher said *whoops, our bad, we didn't know either* and had her sign the correct contract.

Aaron didn't do this on his own, though. There was no gain in that. This was a long-term client who he'd bill hourly regardless of how this one contract went.

If the publisher didn't back down, Sydney wouldn't get the money promised, and she probably wouldn't be able to touch her game, either. Not while the contract was in dispute.

There was no way around that, no matter how desperately Dylan wished otherwise.

24

Sydney was grateful that Josh stuck around. She was on the other side of the emotional chasm now; this feeling was as familiar as the one that came before. Now that she'd moved past her doubt and self-loathing, there was a new voice.

You overreacted.

She was better at ignoring this one. It was typically accompanied by sanity. Josh's being here helped too. His presence was another reminder of the reasons she adored him, and all the things he'd said warmed her from the inside out.

"How are you feeling?" Dylan asked.

Not secure enough to spill her guts to him, but happy he was here. "Heading toward *better*."

He tugged her to her feet, wrapped his arms around her, and pressed his lips softly to hers. "I know everyone says this, but I mean it—if you need me, I'm always here to listen."

"Not everyone says it." But she still made those who did prove it. It was safer that way. "It takes a while to get there, but thank you." She could sink into his embrace, though, and that felt wonderful.

He held her a little longer, then kissed the top of her head before loosening his hug. "I'm going back to our place, to get our laptops. You're in good hands, and I'll be back soon."

"Thank you." She stole another squeeze and brushed her lips over his. After he left, she turned to Josh. "I'm sorry."

Josh crossed the distance between them in a few steps and pressed his fingers to her lips. "You know how I feel about that." He meant the apology.

"And you know I can't help it."

"In that case, apology accepted."

The only thing that would silence the voices was time. But when Josh pulled her close, it helped.

"Thank you." She gripped his shirt in her fists, enjoying having something to hold onto. "Thank you for not walking away today. For pulling me out. For sticking around after. And for whatever comes next."

"You'd do the same for me."

"Except you don't fall into debilitating spirals of doubt."

"But I am an inconsiderate dick sometimes, and you tend to be pretty reasonable, as long as I don't push my luck."

"I love you." She hadn't missed when he said it earlier. "I never stopped, and I don't ever want to."

He smiled that stunning, heart-stopping smile she adored so much. "I'm going to try not to give you any reasons to change your mind."

"I'm not giving up Dylan, though." She didn't want to bring it up now, but it needed to be out there.

Josh shrugged. "Me either. Since that seems to be an all-around sort of consensus, we're good. Hell, I'd say we're pretty wonderful."

With each moment that passed, she felt better. She led Josh to the couch and snuggled into his arms. This was comfortable and right and something she'd missed terribly. She was happy to stay here, curled up against him, feeling him run his fingers through her hair.

When the door opened a short while later, she didn't stir.

"Can I get in on that?" Dylan asked.

Sydney was great with that. "Of course."

He planted a kiss on her lips, and then Josh's, before dropping next to Josh. He tugged Sydney so she was lying across both their laps.

It was just awkward enough to make her giggle. That felt good. She tried to make it work, but gave up quickly. "I appreciate the sentiment, but nope. Not comfortable."

"We'll figure it out." Dylan spoke with so much confidence, she didn't question him.

She wanted to cuddle longer and maybe more. However, an edge of doubt lingered. She didn't want sex to become a way to mask her insecurities. That, and she wanted to find out what happened today with her contract.

"We should get to work." It took more effort than she expected, to say the words.

"All right." Dylan sounded as reluctant as she felt. They untangled themselves, and he grabbed the bags he'd brought back. He set one laptop next to Josh and shouldered the other one.

He set up in the kitchen and flipped his computer open. "Wi-Fi password?"

"You're asking me to make a big commitment with that," Sydney teased.

"I know. And I'm cocky enough to believe we've reached that stage in our relationship."

Sydney grinned. "I'm good with that." She gave him the login info.

"I don't get it," he said, as he studied his screen.

"There's nothing to get. It's a random mishmash of letters and numbers."

"So weird. I love it."

With him at the kitchen table, screen facing away from them, Josh and Sydney set up in the living room. It kept them all within view of each other and let Dylan hide sensitive information.

Dylan was certain about what they'd find, but Sydney had her doubts. If something like this was happening on a wide scale, someone would have uncovered it already.

She searched anyway. First for Aaron Jorgensen. Which, thanks to the Internet assuming she misspelled something instead of wanting exactly what she'd typed, returned pages of personal listings, social media accounts, everything—for anyone whose initials were A.J.

"Clients next," Josh said.

They used the list that was public on the firm website, to make sure he wasn't violating any NDA's. Those were the bigger-name companies anyway—the businesses more likely to have dozens of dealings, and several of them with smaller groups.

Sydney felt frustration sinking in. Everything out there was standard complaint stuff. A massive corporation pissed off a little guy as part of their business model, and the little guy was going to tell the world.

She wanted to reach out to every single one of the people who'd written the blog posts and social media posts, and tell them, *Me too. I feel you.*

And then she hit something that sounded suspiciously like her situation. A person who swore they'd read the entire contract, and when they signed, it wasn't the same.

Then there was another example, and another.

Josh fed the names to Dylan, who used them to focus his search.

It was dangerous, but Sydney felt a spark of hope glowing inside. "What does this mean for me? I might get my game back if this is happening, right?" She felt giddy, speaking the words.

Josh and Dylan's winces mirrored each other.

That was a bad sign.

"Best case scenario, you have your game back tomorrow." Josh's voice was strained. "We call Aaron and the publisher on this, and they say, *Our bad. Let's cancel that whole deal.* It's doubtful they'll still go through with the original terms, but they may."

Her heart sank. "What are the realistic scenarios?"

"Looking at the publisher records, this isn't the first time they've done this," Dylan said. "They'll deny any claim you make. And this will be tied up in court for months."

She could put pieces together from there. "So I can't touch the money, because if lose, I won't get to keep it, and I can't sell my game, because the rights are currently in question."

The downward spiral was rushing back, full force, squeezing like a fist around her lungs and stealing her rationale.

Dylan frowned. "I'm sorry."

"We're here for you, however you need us." Josh rested a hand on her thigh.

"I need to not lose the only source of income I have." She needed to not freak out again, but she might not be able to control that any more than the rest of this.

"Hey." Josh kissed her. "We'll figure it out." His touch silenced some of the voices, but it wasn't a solution.

"We'll take this back to Laurie and see if she's willing to discuss things," Dylan said.

Sydney didn't like that plan. "What are the odds she'll hear you out?"

"We can proceed with or without her. Dylan and I can file the complaint against Aaron. Her life will be easier if she listens and acts appropriately."

Sydney wasn't assured. Laurie obviously had a different definition of *professionally appropriate* than Sydney did. "And if she doesn't see things that way?"

Josh's laugh was strained. "Then she's almost prophetic. She told me you would ruin my career. Not listening to you—to us—could destroy her firm."

"She said that about me?" The ache in Sydney's chest grew. Everything they were doing was supposed to help, but she was feeling shittier and more helpless with each passing moment.

Josh cupped her cheek and held her gaze. "I told you, I choose you."

"Which is why you quit, which means she was right about me." Sydney clenched her jaw. She didn't want to cry. "I don't want to ruin anyone's career. Except the assholes' who screwed me over. I just wanted more of your time."

"I know." He stroked his thumb along her jaw. "This was my decision, not yours. You can't take the blame for it."

Experience said she could, and she would, but Josh made his argument sound so logical…

"I sent Laurie an email." Dylan's tone was kind. "I copied her assistant and asked to get on her calendar tomorrow morning. All of us. I made sure to tell her it was critical."

All of us. That terrified Sydney. At least the fear pushed her clawing doubt aside. "I'm not going to be able to sit still until then."

"Fucking is a good outlet for unspent energy," Dylan said playfully.

She appreciated his levity. She must not be as far down in the pit as she feared. "For the next sixteen hours?"

"Of course not." Dylan shook his head. "We'll need some sleep, and to shower before the meeting. Though, with that shower of yours..."

And she was smiling again. "I'm going to need a little more seduction and foreplay. And I still need answers about what I'll do if I can't have my game back."

"Make a new one," Josh said. He of all people knew that wasn't so easy.

"I SIGNED AWAY A LOT OF MY INTELLECTUAL PROPERTY IN that contract."

Josh shrugged. "But not all of it. There are things they can't touch, and you happen to be tight with the guys who can tell you what those things are."

"It's still not as simple as *make a new game.*" She hated to point out the obvious. Mostly because his idea was a nice fantasy, and she'd rather sink into it.

"But you have concepts." Enthusiasm bled into

Josh's voice. "Dozens of them, and a lot of them are solid enough to grab and build on."

She loved that he remembered that. "I don't know how objectively good any of them are."

"Fortunately for you, you have a test audience." Dylan closed his laptop and joined them in the living room.

"You're so biased," she said.

He settled on her other side from Josh. "I'm glad you know that. We also want you to succeed. Tell us what you have, and let's make this work."

She twisted so she was half-leaning on Dylan, and Josh tugged her legs up, to drape over his. This worked much better than what they tried earlier.

For the next several hours, they bounced around a huge swath of ideas. Sydney wrote everything down. They'd build off a tangent, and then loop back to a previous idea. From fractured thoughts, a discernible image began to emerge.

Sydney found herself laughing more than not. It was easy to fall into this. The entire setting felt natural. How had she gone without this kind of support for so long?

"What about a sex game?" She tossed the idea out. It wasn't a real suggestion, but things were getting silly.

Josh raised an eyebrow. "Like those dice they sell?"

"But more intimate."

Dylan scrunched his face up. "It won't work with just two people, if it's DM driven."

She loved that he was thinking along those lines. "We have three people."

"Do I get to roll the dice, to see if I can enter your love tunnel?" Josh asked.

She winced at the bad phrasing, but she couldn't stop laughing. "With your spear of penetration?"

Dylan gave an exaggerated cough. "You two are horrible. It's *obviously* a pleasure cave."

"I don't know…" Sydney tried to look serious for half a breath, and failed. "*Your barbarian strolls through my pleasure cave,* doesn't sound quite right."

Dylan drew his fingertips lightly up her arm, to caress her neck. "Because you're putting too much thought into it." His voice dropped an octave. "I think it sounds incredible."

She could argue, but she didn't want to. His touch sent too many delicious thoughts racing through her head.

25

Josh was surprised when Sydney pressed a finger to his lips, and pushed him back from kissing her. He quirked an eyebrow in question.

She was smiling though. That delicious, mischievous smile that had earned the nickname *Tink* all those years ago. She looked like a playful fairy waiting to stir up trouble and fun. "If I'm the DM, this is my story."

"So, is that a *no* on the love tunnel?" Josh asked.

"It's not. But I want something else, first."

"Like what?" Dylan looked as curious as Josh felt.

"Don't get me wrong, I love being on display, but I figure there's got to be something to watching, too." Sydney snapped her fingers. "So… get to it."

Josh stared at her in disbelief. "I'm sorry, what?" He finished the question with a laugh.

She waved her hand. "I want to see you two be all sexy and stuff."

"*Sexy and stuff.* Is that the clinical term?" Dylan untangled himself from the three person pile and stood.

Josh needed to put a little more thought into it. "Not that I *ever* would argue about fucking Dylan—sorry, getting sexy and stuff—but I've really got you on my mind, Tink."

She ducked her head, but couldn't hide her flush. "Then I guess you have to get creative about how you use your spear of penetration."

Josh could do creativity. He stood, gripped Dylan's shirt in his fist, and kissed him hard.

Dylan pressed back with enthusiasm, biting Josh's bottom lip, and holding his head captive.

Sydney's breathy gasp was the perfect accompanying music. Josh could see why she liked this being watched thing. At least, with the right audience.

As he deepened the kiss, need snaked along his skin, and chased away the lingering shadows of stress. He raked his nails down Dylan's chest, and received a low groan in return, that hummed against his mouth.

He loved having Sydney back in his life, but just as much, he adored that things were right with Dylan again. Better than right. The way they should be.

Dylan cupped Josh's semi-erect cock through his jeans. He stroked, and Josh hardened under his touch.

Some days, Josh was up for long make-out sessions. He could swap gropes and slide into mutual masturbation, and enjoy every drawn-out moment.

Right now, too much desire flooded his senses. He wanted to be immersed in everything at once.

Josh undid Dylan's pants as he knelt in front of his boyfriend—fuck he liked the sound of that. He worked Dylan free, drawing another delicious groan. When Josh licked along the head of Dylan's cock, he bucked against Josh's touch.

Josh's dick strained against his zipper, begging to be free. He needed release, but it would wait.

He took Dylan in his mouth. Layers of pleasure overlapped, from being responsible for Dylan's moans, and because he could almost feel the touch of lips on his own skin.

He wrapped his fist around the base of Dylan's shaft, pumping in time to the thrust of hips against his face. He flicked his tongue out every few seconds.

As Dylan's thrusts became more insistent, Josh responded with increased enthusiasm.

Dylan gripped the short strands of Josh's hair tight. He fucked without hesitation. He was lost in the pleasure, Josh could tell from his grunts and lack of abandon.

Josh stroked Dylan's sack. Dylan wouldn't last much longer.

Dylan tightened his hold on Josh's hair. Yanking. Pulling. He thrust hard, and a salty spray hit the back of Josh's throat.

Josh continued to lick and suck, until Dylan slowed. He eased up and pulled back, licking Dylan clean as he pulled away.

Dylan pulled him to his feet, still holding his head, and kissed him hungrily. Driving their tongues together. Molding their bodies into each other.

They finally broke apart. "How is that always incredible?" Josh asked.

Dylan chuckled. "Pretty sure that's my line."

"Was that what you were hoping for?" Josh turned to Sydney, who watched them with hungry eyes, her shirt pushed up above her breasts.

She licked her lips. "So much better than. I think we've got a lot of experimenting to do."

"Good thing we've got time." He and Dylan knelt on either side of her. Josh claimed her mouth, and Dylan lowered his head to her breast.

Sydney's whimper was delicious torture to Josh's already aching cock. He glided his hand down her stomach, under the waistband of her sweats. He nibbled her lips and dipped under her panties.

She was slick and wet when he slid between her folds.

"You didn't take care of this while you watched?" he murmured against her lips.

"I was holding out for something to do with a spear of penetration, and a pleasure cave."

Fuck, he loved this woman so much. "I remembered the condoms this time."

"No." She kissed him again. "You don't need to. Neither of you."

They'd had that in their relationship before. Both

of them were clean, and she was religious about taking her birth control.

And Josh knew what kind of trust she was offering up in making the decision again.

Josh wasn't sure how they managed it, but her sweats and his jeans came off, while he and Dylan continued to cover Sydney with kisses.

She straddled his legs, and her gaze met his.

"You're so amazingly beautiful." He stroked her cheek.

She tried to look away, but he held her chin up, needing to see her eyes. "You're just saying that because you're getting laid."

"No." It was true, that feeling of being a third wheel was gone. But as long as he had Sydney in his life, he'd make whatever concessions he had to. "I'm saying it because it's true. You're beautiful and brilliant and loving and everything incredible."

She kissed him in response, devouring his mouth. He poured every bit of love he had into returning the feeling.

When she lowered herself onto his cock, he groaned and dug his fingers into her thighs. Feeling her wrapped around him, warm and tight… this was more than sex. He'd spent so many nights building up what they'd had to this impossible pinnacle.

And this moment was nothing like what he'd imagined. It was better. More pure and complete. It was perfect.

Sydney was drowning in attention, in the best possible way. Dylan kneaded her breasts and sucked on her nipples. Josh slid inside her, rocking slowly. She didn't know where to turn. There was so much to taste and feel.

Josh pulled her face to his for another desperate kiss. It was like he couldn't get enough of her lips, and she was good with that. While he devoured her, Dylan nibbled on her ear, and dragged his fingers up her spine.

He broke the kiss to crush his mouth to Josh's. The sight, and the adoration that flowed between them, sent a spike of desire that tugged in her heart and pulsed between her legs.

Dylan turned back to her, nipping her lips before licking a path back down to her chest.

He slid his fingers around her clit, and she moaned at the new intensity that surged inside. He stroked her swollen button, and scraped his teeth over her nipple.

His touch, combined with the steady thrust of Josh inside her, sent her reeling toward climax. She tumbled into orgasm without warning, gasping at the onslaught of everything.

She didn't know if she wanted to squirm away, or take more, until it was too much.

Josh's groan filled her head. Her thoughts swam

with bliss, and everything flowed into a wash of ecstasy.

Dylan didn't ease up on his attention, pushing her into a second orgasm.

She clenched around Josh when she came, no longer knowing where one of them ended and the next begin.

Josh's frantic thrusts and grunts told her he was on the verge of climax too. He squeezed her legs hard, and for a heartbeat, everything in the world paused.

Then he slammed inside her as he peaked. Filling her up. Leaving her in a blissful haze.

They slowed to a stop, and she rested her forehead against Josh's chest. Dylan trailed his lips along her shoulder.

Whatever came next, the three of them would confront it. And in between, they'd explore each other. Physically. Mentally. All of it.

Sydney was looking forward to each and every new moment.

DYLAN WAS GLAD SYDNEY WAS SLEEPING SOUNDLY. IT had been a long, stressful day.

Which was probably a large part of why he was still awake. He couldn't afford to be bleary eyed in the morning, but knowing that didn't help him shed the tension that thrummed through his body.

He extracted himself from Sydney and Josh, and

wandered into the living room. Maybe sitting out here would help him unwind.

His mind looped over the day's revelations. Why he'd stuck around this morning—because Josh meant so much to him. Because he already didn't want to imagine life without Sydney.

This was all so fucked up. That was what logic said. He shouldn't be involved in this. He shouldn't be willing to share.

Does it matter?

No. Logic didn't matter here. He felt what he felt, for both of them.

"You all right?" Josh's question drew Dylan back into the room.

Dylan glanced at the clock. Had he really been here for more than an hour, just thinking? "Yeah. I'm good." And he was. "Really good."

"Whatcha thinking about?" Josh dropped onto the sofa next to him, pressing his leg to Dylan's.

"A lot of things. You know, if the two of you hadn't broken up three years ago, I probably wouldn't be part of this now."

"Not that I'd know in that case, but I wouldn't want that. There's a weird kind of ambivalence here. I hated that time away from Tink, but I wouldn't give up my time with you."

Dylan agreed. He hated that Josh and Sydney had been hurt, but he wasn't willing to surrender either of them. "So if you could go back in time…" He wasn't sure where the question was going.

"Would I tell myself not to be an asshole? Probably. But if I have a chance to go back and fix things, I'm not only telling me to treat Sydney better, but also to go find you."

"I was going out of my mind this morning, trying to figure out why you'd quit."

Josh sighed. "I didn't mean to add to your stress. I needed time to process."

"And when we got here, you helped Sydney process, too." There was a spark of jealousy over that. Dylan liked seeing it, but he didn't care for being on the outside.

"Your being here, sticking around, helped too."

Dylan smiled. "I love you. I don't know why it took me so long to put words to it, but I want you in my life, long term. I need you here."

"Me too."

Dylan raised his eyebrows, waiting for something a little more heartfelt.

Josh laughed. "I love you too. I'm glad we're in this together—and by *this,* I mean life." He leaned in, searching Dylan's face, then crushed his mouth to Dylan's.

One of the groaned—or they both did.

Dylan cupped his face, searing the moment into his memories—the hard press of Josh's mouth, the heat that flowed between them… He couldn't count the number of kisses they'd shared in the past, but this was different. It was sweeter, and stronger, and promised everything, and didn't deny them anything.

Desire and expectation roared in his veins as Josh's tongue danced with his. He never would have guessed meeting the perfect woman would land him with the perfect guy as well.

The shuffle of feet on carpet drew his attention, and they broke apart.

"I didn't mean to interrupt." Sydney stood in the doorway, wearing an oversized T-shirt that hung just low enough to cover her ass.

"You're not. Ever. Come here." Dylan gestured.

She approached, and when she was within arm's reach, he grabbed her hand and tugged her into his lap. He was in the mood to bare his soul tonight. There was no reason to stop with Josh.

Sydney leaned into the kisses Dylan laid along the back of her neck. His touch was casual and light, but it sent intense tingles racing over her.

"I love this," he murmured against her skin.

Love. It was an easy word for her to use with Josh. Saying it after so long was scary, but they'd said it before. Then again, she was overthinking this moment. Dylan hadn't said the magic combination of three words.

"Love what?" she asked.

"All of this. What we're doing right now. Having both of you so close. Hearing you laugh when you're happy. Seeing you light up with enthusiasm. I love this, and…"

She frowned at the way he trailed off. "What's wrong?"

He shifted her to the couch and stood.

Emptiness rushed in behind her, at the loss of his touch, despite Josh's still holding her hand and listening quietly.

Dylan crouched in front of her, which put him at eye level with her. "Nothing's wrong." He searched her face. "Everything is incredibly right. Except for this bullshit with your game. But us, here and now… It's perfect. I don't want to say this to the back of your head, though."

Her heart lodged in her throat, and she raised her brows, not trusting herself to respond. Could he hear her pulse? She could. It hammered in her ears, muting other sound.

"I love you, Sydney." He kissed her fingertips. "I know it's only been a couple of weeks, and they've been messy ones. And yeah, a lot of people make fun of love at first sight, and this wasn't that. But it was lust, and it's become so much more. I've wanted you since the moment I met you. The more I get to know you, the more I fall into how incredible you are."

The confession sank deep into her, filling her with a warm glow and making butterflies dance in her gut. She wanted to say it back, but she couldn't. Not until she knew she meant it.

"It's okay. You don't have to be there yet." There

was a hint of sadness in his tone, but understanding muted it.

"It's okay?" She couldn't leave it at that.

He winced. "It stings a little. But I say that to be honest, not to manipulate you. I hope you get there, and if you don't, I understand."

She believed the assurance. That was comforting. "I want to get there. I like you a lot. A whole lot. I'm miserable, thinking about you, not being here. I want you in my life. I want to be on your arm and in your bed…"

"The rest will happen as it happens." He brushed his lips over hers.

If he kept that up, love would happen quickly. She kissed him back. There was a tiny stone of longing that asked why she couldn't tell him now. It whispered, *what if he leaves?*

She ignored it more easily than she thought possible. He was here to stay. She believed him and Josh when they said that.

They had enough to worry about, with their meeting tomorrow, without her causing more drama.

Josh should be dreading the day ahead—the meeting with his mother, the lack of employment…

Instead, he felt lighter than he had in… He couldn't remember, but it was while he was still with Sydney. Before law school. Before the reality of expectation fully caught up with him.

Even sitting in the law firm lobby, with Sydney clutching his hand, him having no idea what they were about to walk into, he felt like everything was going to be all right.

"Ms. Hunter will see you now." Her assistant led them to the conference room attached to Laurie's office.

Dylan was seated at the round table. Josh's mom stood at the front of the room, wearing a scowl.

Josh held out Sydney's seat and pushed it back in as she sat, which earned him a deeper scowl.

Good. He picked the chair next to Sydney, which sandwiched her between him and Dylan.

"The *only* reason I'm seeing you is because I know the two of you don't throw around panicky terms like *this is critical* lightly." Mom's voice was tight. "You don't have much time to prove I made the right decision."

Josh was ready to take the heat for this. "Aaron Jorgensen is manipulating contracts. Bait and switch—"

"Stop." Laurie slammed her palms on the table. "I shouldn't have to say this. I thought after my conversation with Dylan, a week or two ago, I didn't need to. The two of you can't be involved in Sydney's contract. I don't care what she told you."

"We know." Dylan nodded. "Conflict of interest. We've been working hard not to cross any lines."

Mom barked a laugh. "*Everything* about this is a crossed line."

"And not just for us," Josh said. "She's not the only one Aaron has done this to. We have proof. Dylan has proof, since I'm not supposed to be in those files anymore."

Dylan slid a manila folder across the table. It contained several of the altered contracts—showing before and after—and associated complaints they'd found online. "All of these tell a similar story to Sydney's. This isn't a one-time mistake. He's got a history of this."

As Laurie Hunter flipped through the printouts,

she paled. "Fuck me." She sank into her seat. "How long… I can't believe… You've tried to tell me he was a problem."

"I thought he was just incompetent." Josh had said it before, but it bore repeating. "This is worse. I stopped pushing, because you weren't listening."

"This could ruin the firm." She scrubbed her face. "I've been sleeping with him. I never…" She exhaled through her fingers, then met Josh's gaze. "I'm sorry for being blind to this. For yesterday. For everything that led up to it. And I'm so grateful you brought this to me, instead of going around me."

Josh wasn't as certain she'd listen as Dylan had been. "I'm glad we didn't have to go around you."

Mom turned to Sydney. "I still don't know that you're a good influence—"

Sydney cringed.

"—but I apologize for the way you were treated yesterday. And that you got caught up in this. I want to make this situation right for you. You can't touch the money or the game, and I can't change that. I can offer other things, though. While Josh's law-school friends may be clever, this isn't a *get your feet wet* kind of case. I'll get you a real attorney, as long as these two promise to step back from this completely. I can't have any more blurred lines." She gestured to Josh and Dylan.

Sydney's smile was tight. "Thank you."

It wasn't peace, but it was a decent ceasefire.

"Now if the two of you will excuse me, I need to talk to my son alone," Mom said.

Dylan and Sydney shook her hand, then Dylan tangled his fingers with Sydney's and led her from the room.

Josh would much rather join them, but this conversation needed to happen.

Mom turned to him again. "Does this mean you're coming back to work?"

"No." The answer flowed out easier than he thought possible. "My quitting wasn't about this thing with Aaron. You know I've never been happy here."

She frowned. "You spent all that time in law school for nothing?"

"No. I'll still use it. I'll still practice somehow. I haven't figured out the details yet." He definitely wouldn't be working for the publisher he'd been eying. Not if this was how they fucked over people they bought from. "Besides, I paid for the schooling. I can waste it if I want."

Laurie almost looked like she was in pain.

"I actually enjoy law," he said. It might not reassure her, but it helped him feel better to say it aloud. "I have to do it for me, though. I can't do this for you anymore."

"I see." She stood, and he did the same. "If you ever change your mind, you're welcome to apply again. And promise me something."

"All right." He shouldn't agree blindly, but he had a feeling it wouldn't be an issue.

"I need you to swear to me you'll step away from this case of Sydney's. Hands off. You know how I feel about her—prove me wrong. But don't fuck her out of her life's work by interfering."

"I promise." That was something he could do with certainty. And maybe, by walking away like this, he could rebuild a healthier relationship with his mother at some point in the future.

SYDNEY WAS GRATEFUL THE MORNING'S MEETING DIDN'T end in a worst-case-scenario, but things were still pretty bad. They left Dylan at the office, and Josh dropped her off at her apartment, before heading home.

He promised they'd be back tonight.

She'd need to book more conventions. At least she had her other merchandise—toys, models, clothes—even if she didn't have her game to sell. She looked at the boxes stacked in a closet, her gut churning. Acid rose in her throat.

She swallowed it down. The situation was what it was. She wouldn't get anywhere stressing about things she couldn't change. What she could do was make adjustments. Hell, she'd start doing freelance, or even get a part-time job if she had to.

By the time Josh and Dylan showed up that

evening, she'd made a billion lists, but doubt lingered inside.

Sydney didn't have a guaranteed next paycheck. She'd lost half her revenue stream. All the plans in the world might act as a band aid, but they wouldn't fix the core problem.

She kissed both guys as she let them in.

Dylan drew his thumb across the lines in her forehead. "What's wrong?"

She spilled everything she'd kept bottled for the last several hours. It felt good to let it out.

"I have another item to add to your list of things that may help," Josh said.

She liked the confidence in his words. "I'm listening, because I need something."

"Having one or two people to share the rent with would take a huge financial strain off you."

His meaning sank in immediately.

She smiled. "Are you inviting yourself to move in?"

"I am. Not just me, but my roommate too. We're kind of a package deal."

Dylan waved.

Her smile grew. "Here, right? After all, that's why we got the place."

"Here." Dylan pulled her close. "We're not giving up that shower."

She sighed happily and relaxed back into him. Maybe things would be all right after all.

Over the next couple of weeks, Josh and Dylan

moved into Sydney's apartment. It felt right having Josh here again. And incredible having Dylan here.

Sydney added more nearby conventions to her schedule—smaller locations she could get to inexpensively and still earn.

Josh didn't have any trouble finding a new job. His mom offered a great recommendation, and he had his pick. He chose a small charity that wanted an on-staff advisor who wasn't looking for a partner-level salary. It meant he worked more nights than he did days, but they were also willing to give him time off, to travel with Sydney.

They were also planning their next game. Getting into the details and building something. Sydney and Josh would have a handful of new samples to take with them for sale in a few months.

Dylan shared all sorts of stories of the fallout Aaron was dealing with. His name was showing up in legal journals. He was facing disbarment. His life was falling apart.

Sydney wished she could have been there, to see Laurie rip him a new one when she confronted him. Dylan assured her that, if the conference rooms weren't soundproofed, the entire office probably would have heard it.

Josh was working late tonight, leaving Dylan and Sydney to hang out at home. The two were cuddled on the couch, half paying attention to the TV.

"Wash," Dylan said. "No contest."

Sydney hadn't seen that coming. "I'm glad you

didn't say Jayne. That might be a relationship ender," she teased. "And Wash is fun and all, but that's who you'd be if you could be any one of them?"

"Were I unwed, I would take you in a manly fashion."

She laughed. "'Cause I'm pretty?"

"'Cause you're pretty."

"So, you like him for the one-liners?" Sydney was trying to make sense of this.

Dylan shrugged. "That's a lot of it, yeah."

She twisted in her seat so she could see him. "You know you're a way smoother talker than he is."

"You take that back. No one has better lines than Wash." His scowl would have carried more weight if he weren't fighting a smile underneath.

She shook her head. "Nope. I said it. I meant it."

"I can make you take it back." He lunged and tickled her, trailing his fingers up her sides. Hitting every sensitive spot he'd discovered in the last several weeks.

She squealed, but didn't try to break away. His touch was as enticing as it was giggle-inducing. "You'll never change my mind," she managed between laughs.

"Fine." His sigh was exaggerated. He brushed his lips over hers and rested his hands on her hips instead. "You've got it all figured out, which *Firefly* character would you be?"

"Inara."

He raised his brows. "Not what I would have guessed."

"Kaylee is awesome, but I'm already an adorably optimistic genius in my own way."

"No arguments here."

"And Mal looks good in a dress, but if I'm going to be someone else, I want to shed some of the emotional baggage."

Dylan seemed to consider this. "You've put a lot of thought into this."

"I'm swapping my life for a fictional character's. It's got to be right," she said.

"If you were Zoe, you could be my girl."

She had to correct him there. "If I were Zoe, you'd be my guy. Which you already are, and I'm not giving you up. Even to be with Wash. But Inara... She's beautiful and exotic and strong. She's confident and knows what she wants and goes after it..."

He kissed her forehead, and her nose. "Sounds like you're already there."

"I'm not—"

Dylan brushed his lips over hers, silencing her protest. He deepened the kiss, and her insecurities flitted away. Each caress of his hands on her skin, or his mouth on hers, danced through her on fairy wings.

She let the conversation fade away in favor of kissing him back. They had so many nights like this. Everything was easier with Dylan.

"God, I love you," she murmured against his lips. It was the first time she'd said it, but the words tasted as incredible as he did.

He grinned against her mouth. "Say it again."

"I love you. So, so much." She liked the sound of it too. It was better each time she said it.

"I love you too." He sucked a line up her jaw, to her ear, and nibbled her earlobe.

A knock on the door interrupted. She groaned in disappointment.

He planted another kiss on her forehead, extracted himself, and went to answer.

"Ms. Hunter." His voice was abruptly professional.

Tension clawed through Sydney, and she sat up straighter on the couch.

"*Laurie* is fine outside of the office."

Since when?

Dylan stepped aside and opened the door wider. "Josh isn't here, but you can come in if you'd like."

"No, thank you." Laurie looked at Sydney and gave her a tight smile. "Good evening, Sydney."

"Hi." Sydney was pleased her reply—brief as it was—didn't come out as a squeak.

"Happy housewarming." Laurie handed Dylan a basked wrapped in cellophane. She stepped past him and approached Sydney. "I've been thinking a lot. About you. About my son. About this entire situation. I haven't treated you right, and it's nearly cost me a great deal."

Sydney's response died in her throat. She couldn't say, *that's all right,* because it wasn't.

Laurie gave her a real smile. "I hope, someday, you can forgive me."

Sydney did have an answer to that. She stood and met Laurie halfway. "I think it's a distinct possibility. And thank you for the gift, for everything you've done, and for raising an incredible son."

"I'm still not down with all of this"—Laurie waved her hand—"but you both look happy, and Josh does too, when I see him. So it's me, who has to figure that out."

They made a little more small talk, and then Laurie was on her way.

The basket was filled with wine, crackers, and cheese. Sydney and Dylan set it aside for when Josh got home.

Sydney settled back against Dylan, on the couch. "Life isn't that bad," she said.

"My life is fucking incredible."

She grinned. "All right. I can't argue that." Affection surged inside—a potent and delicious mixture of love and security and rightness. "Thank you. For sticking with me. For everything you've done. For loving both of us."

He looked at her, brow furrowed. "You don't have to thank me for that."

"I do. Because I'm grateful. I never want to take either of you for granted. And I also want you to know I love you. Truly and completely. For everything that you are, that you bring out in me, and that you make possible in the future."

"I love you too." He squeezed her tight.

God, this was never going to get old. This here, with Dylan and Josh, was incredible. She loved everything about it, and she never wanted to go without either of them.

It tuned out life could be better than fantasy, and the three of them were the perfect proof, as far as Sydney was concerned.

27

Sydney couldn't believe she'd met Dylan at this same convention a year ago. Talk about a life-altering encounter.

Day One was winding down, and she hadn't stopped smiling or talking for most of it. She'd also been on her feet almost that entire time. She was sore and tired, but energized.

"Good opening day." Josh slid up behind her and wrapped his arms around her waist.

She leaned back into him with a smile. "*Fantastic* opening day."

Their new game was selling amazingly well. Even better, last week she'd gotten the official news that *Changelings and Caverns* was hers to sell again. When people saw the board game was available, she'd sold through half her stock.

At this rate, they'd be out before the end of tomorrow. "We'll need to start taking pre-orders for the next print run," she said.

"There are worse problems to have."

"How *dare* you?" A loud gasp cut through the waning chatter in the vendor hall.

Sydney's grin grew, and she scanned the faces for Dylan.

He approached, his scowl wavering. "My best friend and my girlfriend… I can't believe this."

"Knock it off, Mr. Melodramatic." Sydney playfully smacked his arm.

He grabbed her wrist, stepped closer, rather than pulling her away from Josh, and pressed his mouth to hers.

She groaned and sank into the kiss. That still hadn't gotten old, and she couldn't imagine it ever would.

This was the perfect life. It didn't matter what anyone said, or that the three of them had the occasional bump. Sydney wouldn't have things any other way. She couldn't have written a better ending if this was the conclusion to one of her games.

For more second chance angst with a happy ending, read RUNNING FOR IT. Violet put her past with Ramsey behind her for a reason, but when a night of reliving memories lands her in bed with him and his best friend, she has to admit sometimes they were good together. But the people they are in the bedroom don't mesh with the masks they wear for the public.

www.ingramcontent.com/pod-product-compliance
Lightning Source LLC
LaVergne TN
LVHW091039080826
845145LV00002B/558

9781955518680